A Love

AFFAIR FOR

ETERNITY

BOOK 3

C. Wilson

LETTER TO MY READERS

I know I had y'all with the juicy eyes for the way I ended book two, and for that, I do apologize, but this one is just as emotional. So, let me apologize now. With this one, I'm going to break a few hearts before I make it better. I have to trust me, it's needed. I want you to feel how I felt while writing this. I want you to *feel* the emotions. I want to thank all of my readers. Every single last one of y'all. Special thanks to the members of my Facebook reading group: Cecret Discussionz. Like every book in this series... it's time to make that snack run. Pour that drink up. Make sure the little ones are tucked away and make sure your lover knows that you are mentally gone for the night.

Take this ride with me...

-xoxo-

C. Wilson

A Love Affair for Eternity Book 3 Playlist

Could've Been, H.E.R ft. Bryson Tiller

One of Them Days, Kiana Lede

Try Sleeping with a Broken Heart, Alicia Keys

Bitter, Meshell Ndegeocello

Till It Happens to You, Corinne Bailey Rae

Rain, Razah

Think About Me, Dvsn

Fool of Me, Meshell Ndegeocello

Let Em' Know, Bryson Tiller

Promises, Jhene Aiko

Karma, Queen Naija

Touch, Sleeping At Last

Lifetime, Maxwell

Redbone, Childish Gambino

*C*hapter 1

"Can we get him in the car?" Bleek asked.

"I don't know. You think we can get you to the car?" Sha asked the statue of a man on the grassy yard beneath him.

When Bleek saw the flutter of the man's lids open and close repeatedly, he spoke.

"Let's move. Her son is hit we gotta—"

"Who son is what? Ohhhhh my Goddddd Malikkkkkk!"

Bleek looked towards the side of the house and saw Eternity standing there crying. All of this… all of this was too much for him. The backyard looked like a fucking circus show. This was never had how he moved. This was never how he had done things.

In all of his years of pulling off jobs, he had never let his emotions fuel him.

"Ohhhh Malikkkk," Eternity cried out.

When a neighbor's light turned on, Bleek quickly walked over to her. He placed his steady hand over her lips, his palm cupped the lower of her face from cheek to cheek. His other hand cupped the thigh of the infant in his hand. Badly, he was trying to stop the blood.

"Stop saying my fucking name before the neighbors hear you!"
He had to turn that cold switch on. He loved Eternity with everything in him, but he didn't have plans on going to jail for anyone.

This territory that he was playing on wasn't his to toy with. There was no making things disappear at his disposal where he was. He already felt like he was playing it too close by still being on the scene. *We need to make moves and quick.* His thoughts clouded his mind as he removed his hand from her mouth because he saw that she was trying to speak.

"I'm calling out to him... to my baby... that's his name," she whimpered.
Bleek raised his eyebrow.

"Go get back in the car... now." He said through clenched teeth, "we will meet at the nearest hospital. Drive Man-Man's car the rest of us will get in the van. Clean your face when you get in the car. I put blood on you."

Eternity's face started to contort into pain, but Bleek really needed her to be strong.

"Who's blood? Oh my Go—" Eternity started to cry out until Bleek interrupted her.

"Be that girl I met in the Rite Aid parking lot. Be that gutta chick ma. I need you to be strong right now. That's the only way we can save them both."

Eternity looked behind Bleek and saw that Sha was helping Man-Man off of the ground. She shook her head up and down as she agreed with him. Bleek already knew that she was processing it all. It was a lot to take in when he had walked into the yard. The sounds of the whimper of her child caused her to look down at him.

"Save him, Malik." She turned on her heels and then made her way to Man-Man's car. She trusted Bleek with everything in her. She saw her child in pain, and still, with his words, she knew that things would be okay. He was the one that had saved her boy.

As she limped away, tears slid down her cheeks. Still, although her soul yearned to be near her child, she honored Bleek's request. He needed that old Eternity to emerge to handle the situation at hand, and that's what she was going to do. Bleek watched as she walked away.

He needed her to jog, run, something, but he knew that on her injured foot that she couldn't. He turned around and saw that Sha was helping Man-Man walk towards the van. Bleek didn't know Man-Man, but he could tell that his ass was strong. He took a bullet to the neck, and his ass was still standing, he was fighting to stay alive. Bleek knew that it had to be the love the man had for Tori and the kid that he was expecting that kept him holding on.

As he put a pep in his step to make it to the van, he thought of the child that he had tucked in his arm. *She named him Malik, yet she says he isn't mine.* He thought. Instantly, he thought about the ransom note that Vincent had left behind when he first had disappeared with the boy.

ONE MALIK FOR THE OTHER.

The sentence was burning his brain. How did he miss this? He was so preoccupied with saving the child that he didn't see the signs in front of him.

Still not wanting to see the obvious, he chalked the name-giving up to the love that Eternity had for him. He was sure that he knew her inside and out. He was convinced that if the baby in his arms had any ties to him that she would have told him. While still holding the wound in the baby's leg firmly, Bleek held him close. He felt a stiff object inside of the baby's bodysuit.

Through the cotton material, it felt like folded papers, but Bleek couldn't be too sure. There was no way that he was going to stop applying pressure to the wound to find out. He sat in the driver's seat, ready to take off to the nearest hospital. He impatiently waited for Sha and Man-Man to get into the back. The sliding door in the rear of the van closed. Bleek turned the engine on and maneuvered the vehicle off of the street. Sha applied pressure to Man-Man's neck.

"Yo, Siri! Yo, Siri!" Sha was yelling in the back. Bleek sucked his teeth.

"It's... *Hey Siri!*" he corrected.

Bleek's phone beeped twice as it waited to hear his request.

"Direct me to the nearest hospital."

"Starting directions to Erlanger Memorial Hospital..."

Bleek drove with skill only using one hand while he maneuvered the utility van, he held the baby with the other. Keeping with the speed limit restrictions of the construction zone he was passing by wasn't going to happen. As he skillfully maneuvered the vehicle, he prayed that the police wouldn't come out of nowhere and attempt to pull him over. The guns and the two bodies clinging to life inside of the van wouldn't be a good look to a state trooper.

He looked at the SUV in front of him and saw that Eternity was driving way faster than him. If he was doing 80mph, she had to be doing 90.

"How it's looking back there?" he asked Sha.

"Uhh, we good."

"You not sounding too sure."

"His eyes are closed…" Sha said lowly.

"Make sure he stays the fuck up! We're not losing anybody today!" Bleek roared.

Sha shook Man-Man aggressively. Naturally, he was rough. He didn't have that soft side to him. Man-Man blinked his eyes slowly. *I can't believe this nigga shot me,* he thought as he looked up at Sha. He figured that he must have looked bad because although the stranger of a man's face was stone cold, his eyes showed worry.

Sha's face was becoming foggy for Man-Man. He was slowly losing consciousness, and he felt it. He groaned when he felt the pain that was finally starting to set in. *Why the fuck did I even get out that car?* Man-Man thought back to the moments right before he was shot...

"I just can't sit here and not do anything. Vincent obviously isn't himself. He has to be doing drugs again."

Eternity rambled, she was looking for any reason that could explain to her what was going on. Man-Man chewed on his bottom lip as he observed the house that was just two front yards up. The truck they sat in swayed side to side from the weight of Eternity rocking her leg from left to right. She was nervous, and as every minute on the clock in the car passed, she felt like the breath in her body was going.

"If he's off the pills, he is going to kill my baby and both of them." Eternity said before she placed her face into her hands and balled.

Man-Man knew that she was right. In a sober state, Vincent was paranoid. With the euphoria that came with Heavenz, it would only make the paranoia ten times worse.

He knew that if nothing else that his cousin seeing him would let him know that things were real. It was so easy to get delusional while taking the drug. Man-Man knew that his face and his voice would be clarity for Vincent.

"Stay here, and don't get out."
Man-Man unbuckled his seat belt and then turned to exit the car.

"But wait... you don't need to go in there. You have to be here for my sister and the baby. Let me go." Eternity said quickly.
Man-Man sucked his teeth and then turned his body her way.

"Do you know how to shoot a fucking gun?"
He didn't mean for his tone to be harsh, but it had come across like that. He didn't want Eternity to go in the first place, yet there she was.

"No," she whispered.
"Exactly. So, like I said. Stay in the car."

Man-Man exited the car and then lightly jogged down the street towards the house. When he made it to the yard next door, he took his gun out and then held it close to him. With the nose to the gun aimed in front of him, he was ready to let one go if need be.

When he made it to the backyard, everything was moving fast, too fast. Sha was behind lawn furniture taking cover, while Vincent had just burst out of the back door to the house.

Bang...

Vincent shot in Sha's direction. It was clear that he was trying to keep Sha at a reasonable distance while he attempted to make a run for it.

"Vee! Put the gun down man." Man-Man called out. He never lowered his weapon that was aimed at Vincent. He could see that his cousin was rolling, the glossy coat over his pupils and the sweat beads running down his bald head and onto his forehead was a clear indication of that.

Vincent quickly turned in Man-Man's direction.

"You riding with these niggas mayne? Coo..."

Bang...

Man-Man felt a burning sensation in his neck right below his jawline. He coughed and then quickly looked down to see that the right shoulder of his orange jacket suddenly started to become colored crimson from his own blood. With another cough, he felt like he couldn't breathe. In slow motion, he felt like he was hitting the floor. As he was going down, he saw Vincent trying to run away. He let one bullet fly from his peacemaker but didn't know if he was successful.

Bang...

After the shot, Man-Man's gun hit the grass before his body did, and as he looked up at the stars, he felt himself dying. He held his breath because he just knew that as Vincent was running past that he would send another shot his way. He had no doubts that this one would be a headshot and finish the job that he had started.

As Man-Man looked up, his eyes slowly started to close.

"Damn, that's cold as fuck ya own cousin hit you the fuck up. He down, though, that weak ass shot you threw took him down." Sha said as he came into Man-Man's view.

"Shittttt," Man-Man saw Sha hiss, and then he felt pressure being applied to his neck.

"Sha, what happened?" Man-Man heard Bleek's voice, and in his mind, as he felt his breaths becoming shallow, he wondered the same shit.

What the fuck happened? He thought.

"Wake the fuck up, my guy," Sha slapped one side of Man-Man's face while he applied pressure to his neck with the other.

Man-Man's eyes fluttered.

"How far are we from the hospital bro I think we're losing this nigga," Sha said to Bleek.

"We're pulling in now."

The sound of a car horn blaring non-stop could be heard outside of the van. Bleek saw Eternity in the front of the hospital, honking the horn to Man-Man's and Tori's truck repeatedly. She stood outside of the car with the driver's door open. Nurses and doctors started to run out of the hospital to see what the commotion was all about.

"Sha, where's his gun, and where's yours?"

Bleek asked when he saw Eternity flagging down the hospital staff and then directing them to the van that they were sitting in.

"I got both," Sha said.

"Don't walk in with them. Attention is going to be on us."

"Bro, I already know."

Sha had no intention of walking into the hospital with a burner on him. The sliding door opened just as Sha was tucking the two guns behind the car parts in the back. He and Eternity made eye contact, she used her body to block the view of Sha from one of the doctors that had followed her to the car.

Bleek was already out of the car and handing the baby in his arms off to a doctor.

"Please save my baby and save my brother." Eternity cried out as she limped behind the doctors that had her son and Man-Man on stretchers. Sha went to park the van into the hospital garage. After he parked the van, he parked Man-Man's truck into the garage as well.

"Did you call Tori?" Bleek asked Eternity as they and everyone else rushed into the hospital.

"Yes. I didn't tell her about Man-Man... I just couldn't do that over the ph—"

Eternity's voice cracked as tears ran down her face. As her son and Man-Man were being rushed into surgery, she asked God why this was happening to her family, she needed prayer. She needed a miracle to happen. There was no way that a loved one could be taken from her. Her son was innocent, so innocent, and to her, despite the hood resume, Man-Man was a good dude.

He loved her sister with everything in him, and he wasn't afraid to show it. *They will both be fine. They have to be.* Eternity thought to herself as she cried on Bleek's shoulder. She watched as doctors and nurses rushed her loved ones into the back to make miracles happen.

*C*hapter 2

Tori slightly giggled as she watched Man-Man try and pucker his lips for her. He was the first out of surgery. The amount of relief that Tori felt couldn't be measured. The whole cab ride, she sent prayers. The stiffness in her belly made her heartache. She felt like her child knew that something was wrong. The trip to the hospital was filled with anxiety. Her sister had told her that her nephew was shot, but when she asked about Man-Man, Eternity grew silent.

After crying and begging her sister to tell her if he was alive or not, Eternity finally said to her that Man-Man was indeed still breathing. Still, it wasn't a good situation because he was in surgery, and she wasn't updated yet. The last thing that she wanted to do was to raise her child alone but, if something was to happen to him, she was grateful that she had a piece of him to hold on to. She was mentally prepping herself to carry on his legacy. She would teach their kid everything that he had taught her how to be strong and how to think strategically.

Luckily, she didn't have to have those thoughts for long because he had made it out of surgery and was expected to make a full recovery. The kissing noises made Tori smile. He didn't care that his energy was none, he was still his playful self with her. He would always let that stone-cold guard down with her. Just when Tori was about to stand to go and kiss his chapped lips, a voice halted her.

"Marcelo, really?"

Tori looked behind her and instantly grew annoyed.

"What is she doing here?" Tori asked Man-Man, who was lying in the hospital bed in front of her. Her swollen pregnant belly stiffened as the woman behind her slowly walked into the room.

"What is she doing here?" Tori growled again, this time in-between clenched teeth.

Still, she felt like she had a bone to pick with Nova. The thought of the woman got under her skin.

In Tori's mind, whatever still lingered between the woman in front of her and Man-Man was dead and had been dead since the ink dried on their divorce papers.

"I'm here because I am still his emergency contact. How juvenile of you to even expect this man to speak when he was just shot in the fucking neck."

Nova said with disgust as she rounded the chair that Tori sat in and then took a seat at the foot of Man-Man's bed. She didn't give a damn who was inside of the room, nothing was going to keep her from displaying how she naturally felt when it came to Marcelo Bridges.

Their love story was one that had started and ended so quickly that she couldn't even grasp where she had gone wrong. She was taking so many risks by even being in the hospital, but she had to be there. The hollow feeling that she caught in her stomach when she received the call about him being hurt still lingered.

Although she saw with her own two eyes that he was okay, her stomach still had this eerie feeling.

"I was on the jet on my way back to Egypt when I got the call. You move so much better than this. How did you let this happen, Marcelo?" – Nova paused and put one of her fingers up to silence him from responding. – "What do you need from me?" she asked him as she looked deeply into his eyes.

Those dual-colored eyes were what drew her in, to begin with. Momentarily, she got lost in his gaze. From the sidelines, Tori felt sick to her stomach as she watched Man-Man point to the pad and pen that was on the nearby table. She felt the love between the two. She would be a fool to ignore it.

Nausea rumbled in her stomach, which caused her to rub her baby bump. When Nova turned around from the table with the pad and pen in hand, her eyes rolled over to Tori's direction as she handed Man-Man the items. Tori could see Nova's nostrils flare, but the way she held her composure after the brief moment of anger worried Tori. She was content, too content, and that made Tori's mind wander.

While Man-Man wrote onto the pad, Tori watched as Nova gazed at him. She used her left hand to rub Man-Man's shoulder. Her touch looked light like she was scared to apply too much pressure. Tears formed in Tori's eyes when she realized that Nova still had a ring on her finger. It was the most beautiful piece of jewelry she had ever seen before in her life. The cut of the diamond let her know that it had to be custom made. Nova would wear nothing but. She wasn't one of those women that would wear what was available to others. Anything that she had, she wanted to ensure that no one walking the earth had a duplicate.

Man-Man weakly handed her back the pad and pen. Tori watched as Nova silently read what Man-Man had written. Her piercing eyes quickly skimmed the booklet in her hand.

"Okay... okay," Nova shook her head up and down and then ripped the top paper from the pad, "I'll handle it." She said as she made her exit.

Man-Man tapped the side of his bed. Tori's watery eyes looked up. She had been so emotional since she had started her second trimester. At this moment, she wondered how she could compete. *For God's sake, she used to be his wife,* she thought to herself. She felt that she had one up by being pregnant with his child, but the look in Nova's eyes as she spectated Tori rubbing her swollen belly told a different story.

There was a simmering flame in those brown pupils that let Tori know that she could be handled if need be. Nova screamed power. This only being Tori's second time seeing her and still, she felt it. The way Nova walked, her clothing attire, everything reeking off of Nova eluted power. *This bitch said she was on a jet going to Egypt,* Tori thought as she stood in a trance.

The tap of Man-Man's hand against the stiff hospital sheets broke Tori from her daze. He was calling her, and there she was in her head. He needed her more than ever, and she was distracted, emotionally confused, and contradicting her entire relationship. She hated it.

"Tori, get over here."

His raspy voice caused her feet to move. *How juvenile of you to expect this man to speak.* Nova's words sounded in Tori's head. She was allowing the woman's presence to get to her.

"Yes, babe," Tori said weakly.

"I didn't know she was still my emergency contact," he whispered out.

"Shh, please don't strain yourself. It's okay. You don't have to explain."

He gave her a weak smile. She knew that he was tired. He was fresh out of surgery, and as soon as he made it to his room, he was writing orders down. He had workers scattered around the hospital—all to ensure the safety of his child's mother and her sister.

That line of protection went to Bleek and Sha as well. Knowing that Bleek didn't have any other men in Chattanooga, Man-Man made the note that he was good. He was now just as valuable as his family because well, he could tell that after the night they had that, he would become it.

Once Man-Man took a bullet, his thoughts went straight to Tori. As he looked up at the dark night's sky while laying across the same grass that he had installed, he feared not being there for his growing family. The thought of not seeing his child be born rattled his core. As he felt his soul leaving his body, he found the irony in it. The very first income property that he had put all of his tender love and care into was where it would all end for him.

As he felt his life slipping away, everything that he and Vincent had been through plagued his thoughts as well. Then is when he knew that things between the two were always one-sided. Man-Man saw then that Vincent was an opportunist and always had been. Because of Man-Man's father's demise, he found the perfect opportunity to take Man-Man under the wing. He stepped into Man-Man's life at a vulnerable time, and because of it, Man-Man gave Vincent all of the loyalty that he had.

Once Man-Man took that bullet, he promised himself that if he were given a second chance to live that he would never experience the sizzling hot feel of a pellet again. He had too much to live for now. He sniffed away tears as he focused on Tori. The morphine in his system was pulling him into darkness. He needed her face imprinted into his mind to mentally tell him that with every nap, he had reason to wake. He had her love and the child in her stomach to live for.

Tori watched as Man-Man drifted off to sleep. When his fluttery pupils finally closed, her eyes fixated on the pad and pen that rested on the nearby table. Slowly, she walked over to the table. She picked up the pad and then held it up to the light. She could see the perforations on the paper.

Quickly, she took the pad back over to her chair and then dug around in her purse for a pencil. She didn't think that she would be able to pull anything from the pad because she knew that Man-Man was so weak. She didn't think that he had written his message hard enough for her to see anything.

As she dug around inside of her purse for her pencil, her heart was racing. *What could he have possibly asked her to do that he couldn't of ask me?* She wondered to herself. With the pencil, she lightly colored over the page. Like a hidden message, the note started to appear on the paper. She couldn't get all of the message, but she got most of it. Silently, she read to herself.

The income prop on   Rd do a clean-up job.
Vee is dead

Tori's mouth fell open. Still unaware of the events that occurred earlier that day, she was shocked to discover Vincent's demise.

Knock, knock

"Excuse me, mam, my name is Officer Brooks, and this is my partner Officer Harris. We have a couple of questions for Mr. Bridges."

Tori dropped the pad that was in her lap onto the floor because she was startled by the voice that had entered the room. The officer that had just spoken went to reach for the pad to pick it up, but Tori had beat the woman to it.

After picking the pad up from the floor, Tori looked at the two uniformed officers. Just by looking at the two women, Tori knew that they only wanted information on what had happened. Being that the injured people were driven in, she knew that that the officers didn't have anything, but when gunshot victims came through those revolving doors, it was protocol for the hospital staff to call the police. So, there they were.

In her life, she learned early on that the presence of authority was never good, although it should have been. *Shittttt,* she thought to herself when her sister and her nephew had crossed her mind. Being so wrapped into Man-Man's surgery, she wasn't given a chance to go upstairs and mentally check on her sister and Bleek while her nephew was undergoing surgery.

"He literally just went to sleep. You can leave me your card and go." Tori said.
She didn't mean to be rude, but she had other pressing matters to attend to.

The officer that walked in pulled a business card from the chest pocket of her long-sleeved uniform shirt and then walked fully into the room to hand the card to Tori.

"Can I have your name, mam?" she asked as she handed Tori the rectangular card.

"It's Tori," Tori said as she stood from her seat. She crumbled the top paper from the pad before tossing it and the officer's card into her purse.

"Umm, Tori? Did you happen to see Mrs. Bridges?" The leading officer asked.

Tori screwed her face slightly. With the divorce, she figured that Nova would have gone back to her maiden name, whatever that was, but she now had proof that she hadn't. The curiosity and the thirst in the officer's eyes let Tori know that this officer had a wicked agenda when it came to Nova.

"I don't even know who that is," Tori said with a straight face.

The officer put on a small smile.

"I'll walk y'all out," Tori added as she started to walk towards the door.

She stood in the doorway as she waited for the two officers to make their exit. Tori closed the room door behind her and then looked up at the officer who had started to speak.

"Mmm, okay. Thank you. Please do give me a call when Mr. Bridges wakes."

"A huh, now excuse me."

Tori said just before she made her way to the elevators. While walking, she ran into one of Man-Man's nurses. She instructed the woman to not let anyone enter his room unless they were family. Once she had that handled, she quickly rushed into an elevator that was going up. She twiddled her thumbs as she thought about the fate of her nephew.

*QC*hapter 3

Bleek sat in the hospital chair in the waiting room next to Eternity. In his arms, he held her as she cried for hours and then finally slept. The fresh baby's blood still tainted his dark-colored t-shirt, and although he washed his hands to him, they were still infected.

Two female officers had left just moments before wanting to know the story behind their arrival. Luckily for Bleek, Sha was on standby, holding them off. Sha stood off to the side in silence as he just observed the situation at hand and hoped for the best. He was the kind of guy that knew if he couldn't contribute to solving a problem, then his silence was golden. He hadn't opened his mouth until the two officers came trying to pry.

In sensitive situations like this, law enforcement never seemed to understand the severity of privacy. Wanting to open and close a case was their top priority, and how was that fair to families? How was that fair to the mourners? Bleek knew that not too far behind them had to be Child Services, a minor, an infant at that, was injured, and just how the police were called to their location, he knew that CPS was as well. He wished that he could slow up time somehow. Everything was unfolding rapidly, and he knew that it wouldn't end well for Eternity.

He was so ready to put his status into play for her. He knew that with one phone call once, her son was out of surgery and healed that he could have them all out of the hospital and back to Florida. He sat for a while and then mentally toyed with what he should do next. He carefully unwrapped his arm from around the nape of Eternity's neck when he noticed that the doctor had appeared from behind the double doors.

After placing her body gently onto the cushioned bench, he quickly stood and then crossed the room to meet the doctor. He had to be her backbone. He had to be her strength. He had no idea the pain that she was going through because he had no children. He didn't have that emotional tie that she did.

As soon as Bleek and the doctor were faced to face the small built, Indian man looked up to him. The sorrow in his eyes already let Bleek know what it was. Eternity knew that her son had been shot, but she didn't know by the hands of whom. Something inside of him wanted to keep it that way, but he knew that the nobleness in him wouldn't keep anything from her. Not something of this magnitude anyway. Even though he felt like deep down inside, she had been keeping shit from him, he couldn't mimic that betrayal. He loved deeply, and the suspicion of deceit wouldn't change that.

When he had something concrete well then, that could possibly alter his feelings, but as of right now, he didn't have any proof to change how he was feeling. He couldn't picture himself loving Eternity bitterly, even if he did. He took a deep breath as he looked down at the doctor that stood in front of him. He had to put his mental battles to the side to be there in physical and emotional form for Eternity. The lines that creased on the doctor's forehead worried him.

"Give it to me straight."

Bleek had to break the silence because the doctor was openly wearing his nerves on his sleeve. Bleek figured that the man had to be new in his field or intimidated by Bleek.

"The information that I have is privileged. I can only disclose this to the mother and who she deems fit to hear." Bleek flexed his jawline involuntarily. The last thing that he wanted to do was wake Eternity, but he knew that he had to.

"Stay here," he said to the doctor.

Without waiting for a response, he walked further into the waiting room to wake Eternity up. Sha looked up at Bleek to get a non-verbal update. The movement of Bleek, shaking his head from side to side, let Sha know that things were not good. Both men feared Eternity's reaction, so much that Bleek was hesitant with waking her. Bleek chewed on his bottom lip as he gently rubbed Eternity's shoulder down to her elbow.

"Wake up, ma."

He put a little more force behind his rub.

"Eternity, wake up. The doctor wants to speak with you."

Eternity quickly opened her eyes and then stood to her feet. Like a baby deer, she wobbled on unsteady legs. She needed strength, and when she felt Bleek's firm hand on the lower of her back, she was given that. His presence alone was giving her the power to walk.

"Ms. Washington, I would like to talk to you about what happened upon your son's arrival."

"Okay," Eternity said weakly as she grabbed Bleek's hand.

Although she knew that he was right there by her side, she needed to feel him. She held her breath as she waited for the doctor to speak. She feared that the same exact hospital that she had given birth to her baby is where she would lose him. *Lord, please let him be okay,* she prayed, it was something she had been out of tact with for a while now, but she promised that if her son was brought through this that she would search for the religion that she had discovered when she was behind bars. She needed that behind her to pull through this. She needed God to bring her baby boy through this.

"We were successful with retrieving one bullet from his right femur bone. The other wound was a through and through. Therapy will be needed for him to get full function of that leg again."

"Well, then this is good, right?" Eternity showed a little relief in her eyes, but when she noticed that the doctor still had this distressed look on his face, she stopped speaking to let him finish.

"When some test came back that I had rushed to the lab, I see that your son has abnormal white blood cells, he has too many that are damaged."

"What does that mean?" Bleek interrupted.

He hated how doctors always wanted to narrate a story before they got to the ending.

"Get to the point doc. Is he good or not?" Bleek asked.

Eternity squeezed Bleek's hand tighter.

"He has tested positive for acute lymphocytic leukemia."

"For what?" Eternity cried out, "I had him here in this hospital! How did no one catch this? Or is this something that he developed?"

Bleek grabbed Eternity's arm because she had jumped in the doctor's face. It was evident that she had made the man nervous. Either her actions or the deadly stare that Bleek was giving him made him obviously uneasy. He took a slight step back to create some space between him and the couple.

"I can compare notes with his pediatrician here. I do apologize for this, Ms. Washington. We will try our best to find exactly when he could have been diagnosed, but judging by testing, he seemed to have this for a little while now. Going forward, we will be sure to give the best treatment that we can. He's okay for now, but I won't lie to you. This healing will be touch and go. His illness will make it very hard for a speedy recovery. Also, we will need to do a blood transfusion and possibly a bone marrow transplant to ensu—"

"You're saying a fucking lot. Can she see her kid? That's the only thing I want you to answer next." Bleek interrupted the man.

"Yes... can I see him?" Eternity wiped the snot that covered her upper lip with the back of her hand, "can *we* see him?" she asked the doctor.

She included Bleek without even asking him. Being one that held the baby close after him being harmed, Bleek wanted to see him anyway. The doctor who had just delivered the news showed them to the room where the baby was, and then he went on his way.

"You go, ma, I need a little minute," Bleek said as he held the hospital room door open for her.

She raised her eyebrow and then looked him deeply in the face. She studied his features. Stress was aging him overnight, and she hated that she had to be the one to do it to him. He was troubled, and she knew that it was all on her. It had to be the stress that she had unintentionally added to his life that made him look so disheveled.

"No, we will go in together."

Bleek let go of the door and then let it gently close. Why couldn't she just give him the privacy that he had desperately needed?

"I don't see how he could shoot a damn baby. An innocent baby, a baby he raised." She wondered out loud. Bleek looked over to her and saw the tears building in her orbs. Those brown pupils were filled with pain. Pain that he had mistakenly put there.

How was he to know that the baby was strapped to a dead man in that chair? When only trying to defend himself and save the baby, it turned the wrong way, the tragic way. The sound of the baby crying filled his ears. It felt real, so real. So much so that he looked into the room to make sure that the baby was still sleeping.

This shit was taking a toll on him. Suddenly he looked into Eternity's eyes and saw the damage that the situation was putting on her. Bags under her eyes let him know that she hadn't slept. Who would? What mother could sleep after having their child kidnapped and then shot? Even if their body shut down and forced them to sleep, it wouldn't be a peaceful one.

Although Bleek thought that he was moving strategically, he knew that it couldn't be. If he was, how could he shoot the baby not once but twice?

"How could he do this to someone he raised?" Eternity's voice broke him from his thoughts. He saw that she reached for the wall in front of them for support.

"Ma, I don't think he shot him."

Eternity turned around to give Bleek her full attention. What the fuck did he mean, he didn't think that Vincent had shot her son? It was evident by the two bullet wounds that had pierced her little boy's body. He was indeed shot. If not by his abductor, then by whom?

"What do you mean?"

Bleek took a deep breath before he let everything out in one saying. There was no need to take his time with what he was about to say because the blow would hit the same either way. The pain that she would feel wouldn't lessen if he decided to deliver the news slower.

"When I entered that house, he was crying. His cry had so much pain in it, ma. The only thing I was worried about was getting to him. The only thing that I was worried about was saving him."

He paused to sniffle. He was weakening by the second. His confessions were coming out, and it wasn't easy.

During his brief intermission, he noticed that at the time of trying to save the baby, he wasn't moving strategically at all. He was running off of emotions. The old Bleek, the young Bleek, would handle all of his jobs the same. Without care, if bodies dropped, then fuck it, bodies dropped. When his old way of doing things was the cause of his old fling, Toya's best friend, Leah, dying he knew that he had to take a step back and look at himself.

He had to evaluate his pop shit off without remorse mindset. That was the teenage Bleek, even the early 20's Bleek. This Bleek fuck that, this Malik was tapping at 30's door, so he did things so much more differently. *How could I do everything right, and shit still ends up fucked up?* He wondered, which angered him.

"You were worried about getting to him, okay. Tell me the rest..." Eternity pushed.

He didn't realize that he had gone into his head until she spoke. He put his hand on the back of his neck and then moved his head from left to right before clearing his throat. He had to knock the tension out of his body before he continued.

"That nigga shot at me twice, so I shot back twice. Somebody was sitting in a chair towards the back door, I made that my target. I didn't even notice that the cries had stopped with my two shots. How come I didn't notice that? Hm? God, I need the answer.... Please."

Bleek's voice was breaking, and Eternity's heart started to beat out of her chest. He didn't even have to wholeheartedly say anything, she got it. She understood. She got the message loud and clear. Now, she knew that he was responsible for her son getting shot.

She watched as he broke down next to her. Tears. This beautiful man, this protector next to her, was falling apart at the seams. She wanted to tell him then that the baby was his, but she knew that it would only cause him more heartache. Then he would know for a fact that he had brought physical pain to a piece of him. At the moment, she didn't feel like he could handle that. She rubbed his back gently.

His strong arms spread out, and his hands were flat against the wall in front of them. Eternity focused on the tiled floor beneath them and could see his tears hitting the floor as his head bowed. He was whispering, mumbling, and to the looking eye, he looked to be praying, but Eternity knew him better than that. He knew of God, but he didn't know God.

In a situation like this, she knew that he would question their creator's motives. How could God put a baby in harm's way? She wondered the same. Eternity knew that he was talking to himself. He was such a strategic mover that she knew that in front of her, he had to be verbally retracing his steps to figure out where he had gone wrong.

"You were trying to save him," she said barely above a whisper.

He looked to her with his red, tear-filled eyes. How could the tone in her voice sound so understanding? He didn't get it.

When he spat out his confession, he silently braced himself for her blows, for her yells, for something, but instead, she stood next to him calm. If she held hatred in her heart for him because if it, he couldn't detect any. She grabbed his chin and then lifted his head so that he could look through the glass and into the room where their baby was sleeping. The anger in her couldn't be mad at Bleek. She blamed this whole situation on herself. She was sure that if she were more upfront with her own secrets that they both wouldn't be here right now.

She briefly envisioned how life for them would be right now if she would have told him about his child. They would be on his estate in Florida, both enjoying the joys that came with being a first-time parent. Her eyes misted at the could have been, and then she sniffled to push those dreams into the back of her mind. It couldn't happen, how could it? Once she told him about the paternity, she knew that things would crumble.

"Look in that room. You brought him back to me. You saved him, and I know that right now you may not feel that way, but he's breathing, he's here. We have a long road ahead, but today he is here."

She gently held his chin in her hand as she made him look. She made him see that things for right now we're okay. They would worry about the other bullshit later, but right now, they could breathe a little.

She saw his eyes start to warm as he looked through the glass. The tears in his eyes dried as he smiled slightly. He held so much love in his glance, and he didn't even know that the baby that had his attention was his child. *I need to be smart when I tell him,* she thought to herself. She knew how quickly the love in those eyes could turn into hate.

"You did good, you hear me?" she added.

She was praising him like a parent. She was speaking good deeds into his body. She was filling his confidence bucket by reminding him of the good that he had done. Damn, she was such a mother. Instantly, it made him want to seed her. Or had he done so already? He needed a moment to himself. He wanted badly to ask her again about the child's paternity, but he wanted to be easy on the topic, especially with no valid proof. She had given him her word before, so for right now, that had to be good enough.

"Thanks, ma. I'm good. Go ahead and spend some time with him. I'll be in there in a minute."

He used his hand to wipe his face clean. For a moment, he felt like he could breathe a little easier. Eternity nodded her head and then entered the room. Through the glass, he watched her. She walked over to the crib that was in the room and then looked down into it.

Bleek could tell that she was holding onto the crib's railing for support. The way her back hunched over and her head hung low, let him know that she was trying to keep it together. She had her son taken from her, had her son shot, and now she was informed that he had cancer in his blood that could be the possible death of him. He didn't know how she was still standing on her own two feet. At that moment, she was indeed the strongest person walking the earth to him.

He inhaled and then looked to the hospital's ceiling to exhale in a sigh. Loving Eternity came with this. He now felt like it was *his* responsibility as well. He had to be there for Eternity and her son. He knew that whatever treatment was needed could be costly. Without any doubts, he was prepared to foot the bill, he was ready to be there for the boy's treatments. He was ready to be that father figure in that boy's life. All because of the love that he had for the boy's mother.

Bleek looked back into the hospital room and saw that Eternity's back was heaving up and down. *She needs me.* He thought. As soon as he went to open the room door, someone spoke to him.

"Hey, excuse me, dad?"

Bleek turned to his left and saw a housekeeping employee that was in charge of transporting patients around the hospital. They were also in charge of the patients' belongings.

"Dad? I'm sorry, are you a family member?" The woman asked.

"Yes," Bleek answered without hesitation.

He had all intention of stepping up and playing that fatherly role, and that started from now.

"Here you go," she handed him a clear hospital plastic bag that had folded papers inside of it. In permanent marker, he read on the label that it said Washington.

"They had to cut him out of his clothes, so they are still in the operating room to be disposed of. If you absolutely need them, I can try and get them for you, though."

The woman slightly licked her lips, and instantly, Bleek became annoyed. Even on Eternity's worst day, the woman standing beside him couldn't hold a candle to her.

"Yeah, do that for me," Bleek responded.

He would have told the woman anything to get her out of his face. He knew that Eternity would want the clothes that her son was wearing. The woman turned on her heels and then made her way to go get the soiled items that Bleek had requested.

Once she walked off and had given Bleek his privacy, he drew his attention towards the hospital bag that she had given him. Curiosity made him wonder what the folded papers could have been. He just knew that it was probably hateful letters from Vincent signed to Eternity. As he watched Eternity go through the motions inside of the hospital room in front of him, he knew that he couldn't let her read whatever it was. He wanted to, though.

He yearned to know what in the world could have made that man hate the woman that he loved. Or, once had loved. What would make that man hate her so much that he would steal his own baby to put in harm's way? When he opened the seal to the zip lock bag, the smell of blood filled his nostrils. His phone vibrating in his pocket stopped him from pulling the folded papers out.

Paris

He looked down at the name and then forwarded the call to his voicemail. He hadn't spoken to her since he had put her in a cab at the airport. A piece of him felt bad for ignoring her all of this time. As he peered into the hospital room in front of him, he felt it. Eternity was no good for him and probably would never be. Where her life was an emotional rollercoaster Paris' was peace.

Her life came with no conflict, and still, he chose the chaos. He openly decided to put himself through the wringer. Every single time and only for her. He felt like he had been running since he touched down in Chattanooga. When putting Eternity first, he always was feet planted on the ground running. Whatever she needed, he was there. His phone vibrated in his hand one more time. He checked his text messages.

Paris: I hope all is well, the last time I saw you it didn't look like you were in a good headspace. Malik... I'm here if you want to talk about anything.

Bleek quickly read over the message. He had missed calls and text messages from Ty as well, but everyone else would have to wait. He had to give all of his attention to Eternity, especially right now.

After putting his phone back into his pocket, he took that bloody packet of paper out of the hospital bag. The folded paperwork had started to dry shut from the blood. Carefully, Bleek pulled the paper apart.

Vincent Dubois paternity results: 99.999% not the father to Malik Renmen Washington

Over and over, Bleek read the paternity results. The bold letters looked like they were jumping off of the paper.

Bleek knew that Eternity had named her son Malik and at first, he was flattered by it, up until now. The man that had been in the boy's life since birth wasn't his father. Then there was the name Renmen. That name had cultural ties to him. With twenty-five percent Haitian heritage, he knew that Eternity was well aware of the meaning behind that name.

Instantly he remembered that while holding the child, he felt like there was something stiff inside of the child's bodysuit.

"She named him after me because she must have thought that he was mine. He gotta be mine." He whispered to himself.

Ever since he had seen Eternity at the pizzeria a few months ago with the newborn, the thought constantly plagued his mind. As he looked through the room's window and watched Eternity rub her son, their son's hand, his anger started to grow. To him, all of this could have been prevented if he would have known about the possibility of him being a father, he hated being in messy situations, and to him, that's precisely what the case was.

"I shot my own fucking son," he mumbled to himself.

As he watched Eternity pace, the room slowly, his vision became blurry, to him, Eternity had robbed him of fatherhood. To him, it was her fault that their son was laid in a hospital bed. Bleek ground his teeth together to try and keep his anger at bay. He knew that right now was not the time to explode. Still, with him carrying the weight of what he had done, he cared about her feelings. He still put her first.

"Na, fuck that! If he is mine, then I have to know right now!" Bleek growled to himself before he walked into the hospital room.

He tightly gripped the paperwork in his hand.

"Come, step out the room. Let me talk to you." Bleek said sternly.

Eternity raised her eyebrow.

"I'm not leaving his side right now, so speak."

Bleek's nose flared.

"Is he my son?" he questioned.

"Yes..."

Although Bleek was expecting that same answer, still the fact gut-punched him. He placed his hand over his face and then shook his head from left to right.

"I wanted to tell you I swear I did I wante—"

Bleek silenced her with the raise of his finger.

"None of this would have ever happened had I known the very second you pushed him out. You had a whole pregnancy and was playing house with a whole different nigga. For God's sake, you named him after me, Eternity! You robbed me of the experience that comes with being there for your pregnant partner. You robbed me of his fucking birth. I need a test done right now! Matter fact..."

Bleek went to the door and then opened it. He saw a nurse walk by, and he grabbed her gently.

"Yes, sir?" She asked nervously as he ushered her into the room.

"Please page his doctor or whoever you have to. I need a DNA test done right now, and I need the results rushed!"

The nurse looked towards Eternity. When Eternity shook her head up and down lightly, the woman left the room to put in Bleek's request.

"Obviously, I've been treating you wrong all these years. You had the next nigga raising my fucking kid. Do I not treat you with respect?"

Eternity went to respond, but Bleek spoke instead because, to him, the question was rhetorical. He didn't need her to answer a question that he already knew the answer to. He knew damn well he treated her well over the years, sometimes too well.

"Hell yeah, I treat you with respect! Yet you can't fucking respect me. Before any of this had even happened, I asked you..." – Bleek's voice started to crack, but he held it together. – "I asked you was he mine."

Knock, knock

Bleek quickly ran his hand down his face and then turned to the door.

"How is he doing?" Tori asked as she stepped into the room.

"Tori step out. Let me finish this conversation with your sist—"

"She knows…" Eternity whispered.

Bleek looked over his shoulder at Eternity.

"She knows?" he scoffed.

"I'm sorry I know what?" Tori asked as she tapped her fingertips along the side of her thigh.

She felt the tension in the room. She had felt it upon her walking in, but still, she needed an update on her nephew.

"You know that this is my son…"

Before Tori could say anything, Bleek flipped over the table that was in the room. Her answer was written all over her face. With his statement, a sadden expression had slowly started to appear on her profile.

Their son started to cry because of all of the commotion.

"Malik!" Eternity screeched.

She rushed to the side of the crib to try and comfort the crying baby. Without knowing how to adequately address the situation, Tori stood on the sideline and watched the whole thing play out.

The baby crying to Bleek was a constant reminder of the exact moment that he had shot his son. At that moment, he heard this same cry, and then as soon as the two silent bullets erupted from his peacemaker, the noise had ended. The cry had halted, and he didn't even notice it at the time. *How the fuck is this fair?* He wondered as he paced the floors in front of the two women.

Eternity's attempt at getting the baby calm was failing. Still, he was crying. *Why didn't I notice when the crying first stopped?* Bleek's thoughts were running a mile a minute. He wanted his feet to move at that same pace. He wanted to run, he tried to run away from it all. The guilt in his chest felt suffocating, and suddenly he felt like he couldn't breathe. With balled fists at both sides of his head, his breathing felt harbored.

He focused his sights on the tiled hospital floor to try and gather himself. He felt the tears building in his eyes and pressure on his chest made it hard for him to swallow his own saliva.

"He won't stop crying. Tori, please get a doctor…" Bleek heard the worry in Eternity's voice. Still, he couldn't snap out of his trance. *I did this shit.* The very first time he heard the cry of his son was when the baby was in harm's way.

He wasn't even given a chance to hear his first cry upon him entering this world. How could she rob him of that? How could she, for months, deny him his right to be a father? He was supposed to be that protection. For his, he would burn down cities. For his, he would throw his life on the line to ensure that his blood was good. How could she not tell him? *How could she do this to me?*

"I can't do this shit," Bleek mumbled before he made his exit.

"Malik!" He heard Eternity calling out to him.

The distress in her voice would have normally frozen him, but he didn't stop his feet from moving. He couldn't. *Not now,* he thought to himself. The sound of the baby crying grew distant, and the further away it was, the more relief was brought to Bleek. As the sound of his son crying faded, he felt like a coward because he could breathe a little easier.

Chapter 4

Walking through the waiting room to make his exit, Bleek breezed past Sha.

"Yo bro..."

Sha stood to walk out with Bleek but halted when Bleek spoke.

"I just need a minute... please."

Sha shook his head up and down. He didn't know what had transpired in the back, but he could see the stress written all over Bleek's body language. His shoulders hung over, and his bushy eyebrows were scrunched in anger.

His eyes held pain, pure pain, personal pain. The shit looked deep. It was too much, and Sha couldn't relate. He didn't allow himself to open up to feel the kind of disarray that he was witnessing. It had been so many years since he had felt pain like he was seeing. The look in Bleek's eyes gave Sha no other choice but to give him his space.

"Okay, I'll stay here. Go and get your head right."

Bleek finally made eye contact with Sha. He was appreciative of him because, in his life, he had only come across one friend that was of the same makings of Sha. He had only considered one other man on Earth as a brother.

"Thank yo—"

"There's no need, now go," Sha said as he nodded his head towards the elevators.

As Sha turned around to go back to his seat, Bleek bit his bottom lip, and his nose flared—an attempt to keep the tears from falling. He made his way to the elevators to get to the main floor. When he walked out of the hospital, the breeze from outside was refreshing. As soon as the fresh air danced across his face and he inhaled, he felt the contents of his stomach come up. With his hands placed on his knees, he threw up. His back arched as more came up.

"Sir, are you okay?" A doctor walking in to start shift asked.

After wiping his mouth with the back of his hand, Bleek responded.

"Yea, I'm good."

"You sure?" the man asked.

"I said yea, now get the fuck outta here."

The white man raised his eyebrows in shock, shrugged his shoulders, and then turned to walk into the hospital.

"Fuckkkkk!" Bleek roared.

He started to walk out of the lot of the hospital. He didn't realize how long he had been in the hospital until he saw the morning sun beginning to make its peak. He walked down the closest major road he saw. The morning's sunrise brought out the joggers. As he wandered aimlessly, he could feel the eyes of strangers on him, but he didn't care. When he saw the golden arches in the sky, his travels ended. He never was the kind of guy to indulge in McDonald's, but he needed somewhere to sit to clear his head.

When he walked into the establishment, all eyes were on him. His black hoodie covered the baby's blood that was on his shirt, but the throw up on the sleeve of it and his drained facial expression told a story of its old. Bleek took the seat closest to him and then sat it in, after putting his arms on the table in front of him and folding them, he placed his face into the fort that he had made.

"Long night?"

Bleek lifted his head to see an Mc Donald's worker with a spray bottle in his hand.

"You have no idea," Bleek said as he grumbled.

"Do you want a coffee or a tea?" the man asked.

"Na."

"Well, you *can't* just sit here so..."

Bleek raised his eyebrow as he looked the young man up and down. He knew how fast food establishments worked, but still, he wanted to be left alone. He could see that the boy was young, he couldn't have been any older than twenty-one.

Bleek lifted slightly in his seat and then went to go inside of his pocket.

"Whoa, whoa buddy. I mean like you can sit here you don't have to do what you're about to—"

"Shut the fuck up…" – Bleek pulled his wallet from his pants and then took out a twenty-dollar bill – "here." He handed the worker the money.

"Charge me for a tea, I guess, and keep the change. Now get the fuck away from me." He added.

The corners of the young boy's mouth turned upward as he took the bill from Bleek's hand and then scurried away. Bleek sat back into his seat and then threw his head back in a sigh. He was exhausted. His phone vibrating in his pocket caused him to lift his body from the bench again to retrieve it.

Sha

Bleek quickly slid the bar on his screen to answer.

"Tell him to get the fuck back here! Oh, my God! Why would he leave..."

Bleek heard Eternity crying and yelling before he could even say hello. He stood from his seat and then headed out the door.

"Talk to me, bro."

Bleek said as he jogged back to the hospital.

"I don't know where you are, but you need to get back here a.s.a.p. They are trying to resuscitate him but..."

Sha let the last word of his statement trail off.

"But what?"

Bleek asked as he took off running. The fatigue that he was just feeling meant nothing. He raced down the road as quickly as he could.

"But what?" he asked again, this time with his voice cracking.

Bleek could see the sign for the hospital, but he knew that he wouldn't make it in time.

"He's gone, bro," Sha whispered into the phone.

"My baby!" Bleek heard Eternity cry out.

Bleek stopped running and then doubled over in pain. Tears streamed down his face as he breathed sporadically to try and catch his breath. Besides the run that took his breath away, the news was heart-stopping. He leaned up against the silver gate to Lincoln Park as he groaned.

"Fuck! Fuck! FUCK!" he said repeatedly.

Just as quickly as he learned of his newfound title, it was snatched from under him.

"Where are you going?"

Bleek heard Sha say. His mouth sounded like it was away from the phone.

"Aye... you can't let this girl leave. What kind of shit is this? Yo, Bleek, her sister is letting her leave."

"What? I'm coming," Bleek said just before he hung up and looked towards the hospital.

He started to run again. He cut through the parking garage, and when he made it to the entrance of the hospital, he didn't see anyone. *Good,* he thought inwardly.

Although he still couldn't catch his breath, he jogged to the elevators. He mashed the button with his thumb so many times that he felt like he had jammed his finger. He didn't even wait for the people to exit before he rushed into the steel box. Pressing the number eight-button, he waited impatiently as the elevator stopped at all of the floors in between.

As soon as he made it to his floor, he rushed out of the elevator. He saw Sha and Tori in the waiting room. Sha had Tori in his arms. His facial expression looked awkward, and his body looked stiff as he gently rubbed Tori's back. He wasn't into the showing affection thing, but once Eternity had rushed out of the hospital, Tori needed someone to hold her. She couldn't chase behind her sister, and considering what had just happened, she wouldn't.

"Where is she?" Bleek asked.

Tori broke her embrace from Sha and then ran over to Bleek. He held his arms out for her to run into his strong arms, but still, his eyes scanned the waiting room for Eternity.

"I don't know. Why is this happening to us?" Tori questioned.

Bleek took a deep breath and then bit his bottom lip. He knew that Eternity was gone. Being that he didn't bump into her while rushing into the hospital, he knew that she must have taken another exit out of the hospital.

"Is he still in the room?" Bleek asked.

"Yes," Tori whispered as she held him tighter.

"Sis, I need to…" – Bleek's voice was cracking – "I need to say goodbye."

Tori shook her head up and down and then let go of Bleek. She had already said her goodbyes when her sister had escaped from the room. After clearing his throat, Bleek made his way to the room. His feet felt like cement blocks as he walked. He peered into the room to see a nurse wrapping up equipment. He walked into the room without knocking because that boy in the bed was his, all his. The white bodysuit that the hospital had dressed him in after his surgery made him look angelic.

"Sorry for your loss." The nurse said as she watched Bleek slowly approach the bed.

She held sympathy in her eyes. Pure compassion, the words left her mouth with emotion. She was present when Eternity went through the motions, and something inside of the woman told her that the man in front of her was the father. Besides the striking resemblance between him and the baby in the bed, the pain that was sketched on his face was one that only a parent would have.

"Can I hold him?" Bleek asked the nurse.

"Yes, of course. I'll give you your privacy."

Bleek looked at the woman and then shook his head up and down to say thank you. When she left, he placed his strong hands on the side of the bed and then bowed his head. Bleek wasn't the praying type, so he wasn't about to start now. He wondered how God could take something so small and innocent. At that moment, he blamed no one but himself. In his mind, it was a father's job to protect his children, to protect his family, and he felt like he had failed horribly.

"I'm sorry little man," Bleek whispered.

Without it being his fault, he wasn't there to see his son take his first breath, but he could have been there for his last. He regretted how earlier in the day he had let his feelings get the best of him so much that he left the hospital. His firstborn was the mirror image of him. The dark smooth skin complexion, the thick eyebrows, and thick hair, the baby even had a spade-shaped nose like him. Bleek leaned over and then scooped the baby into his strong arms.

He vowed to himself that the lifeless baby in his arms would be his one and only. Never in his life did he want to feel this pain again. He knew that having children brought the upmost joy into lives, but there was no way he would take a chance of heading down that road when possibilities like this one lingered in the shadows.

How could any pain come from something that was supposed to bring so much joy? To him, the possibility shouldn't have even been possible. It was unfair, and he knew that life, in general, was unfair, but when it came to children, he somehow wished that every single child walking earth could have some form of blanket of protection draped around them. All of this, he thought of as he swayed slightly from side to side with a little piece of him in his arms.

He held the baby close to his body and then dropped his face into the crook of the infant's neck to get his scent. As he inhaled, his emotional barriers broke. The boy smelled exactly like his mother. That vanilla scent was so strong that it lingered into his pores. Even after being away from his mother and being held captive by Vincent, he still smelled like her. To Bleek, that smell was supposed to be his happily ever after. A life with Eternity at his side with their child.

"I'm so sorry little man." Bleek cried out as he swayed from side to side.

Anger bubbled inside of him as he thought of everything that was taken from him before he was even given a chance to experience it. He knew for a fact had he known about him being a father that none of this would have happened. He would have made sure of it. Still, he blamed himself because the possibility steadily swam around in his head. To him, if he really wanted to know, he would have put in more effort to find out.

Out of his peripheral sights, he saw that someone was entering the room. So hopeful he turned around quickly because he expected that it was Eternity. When he saw a short Indian man with a clipboard standing in the doorway, his eyebrows dipped in anger. He already knew what this was. It was time for the organ snatchers to make their rounds. He hated how hospitals operated. It's like the workers didn't even wait for the soul to leave the body before they came begging for organs.

"What the fuck do you want?" Bleek growled. He wasn't in the mood to be professional or hold his tongue.

"Urm… sorry sir, but I came to ask about this child's organs. Although he was very sickly a lot of his organs are still very much viable, and there are oth—"

"Enough!"

The man jumped at the base in Bleek's voice. Bleek had heard enough as soon as the man used the word *sickly*.

"Wasn't shit wrong with my fucking son!" Bleek yelled.

While still holding the corpse in one hand, he quickly walked over to the man and then yoked him up by the collar with his free hand.

"You hear me?"

Tears streamed down Bleek's face. As he tightened his grip around the man's collared shirt, the tightness in his jawline intensified.

"There was nothing wrong with my boy!" His voice broke as he defended what was his.

"Bro let go of him. Think about ya seed. You can't put him to rest if you're in jail."

Bleek looked over the man's shoulder, who he had in his grasp and saw Sha standing there. Bleek's eyes rolled over to the man who he had hemmed up, and he saw the fear in him. He let go of the man and then pushed him out of the room.

"Don't bring ya ass back in here and make sure none of ya coworkers come in here either. The answer is fucking no!"

Shaken with fear, the man held the clipboard close to his chest and then shook his head up and down before he scurried away.

"How am I going to do this funeral shit without his moms yo. Where the fuck did she go?"

Bleek had pleading eyes as he basically begged his friend for answers. He knew that Eternity would resurface. She had to. Besides him knowing that she didn't have the means to care for herself, Bleek knew that she would want to be present for her own son's funeral service.

"She gotta wanna be there, right?" Bleek asked Sha in a shaky tone.

"Yea, she gone want to be there," Sha said reassuringly.

Deep down inside, he wasn't too sure about his statement. He had seen Eternity mourn her son inside of that hospital room, and the scene was something that he would probably never get out of his head. It was honestly something that he had wished he didn't see. The moment seemed private as if it were only privy to immediate family. But there he was, an extended family member of an extended family member.

He had witnessed Eternity at her worst. He saw a piece of her die when the boy flatlined. It was like as soon as a doctor informed her that despite all their efforts, it was nothing that they could have done to save the boy is when he physically saw a switch with her.

Sha didn't even know her, but he knew pain, in his younger years he had lost enough loved ones to know exactly what that dark mode switch looked like. With stain cheeks, he watched her slowly walk out of the room. He knew that she would be leaving the hospital.

Everything in him wanted to stop her from leaving. He tried to hold her there at the hospital until Bleek arrived, but he knew that he couldn't. By the look on her face, he knew that nothing could hold her. The same facial expression she had almost an hour ago is the same facial expression that Bleek wore in front of him.

Sha felt for his boy as he watched Bleek cry over the lifeless baby that was cradled tightly in his arms. Sha sighed as he thought about the rest of the days to come. There was no way that he would be going back to Miami when he knew that Bleek needed him.

Chapter 5

Man-Man sighed as he sat up in the hospital bed. He had just got the news about Eternity's son. When it rains, it pours for real, and he couldn't wrap his mind around why everything was happening back to back. Why was everything happening to them?

A few hours prior, Tori had rushed into his room, balling her eyes out. She explained how her nephew was gone, and now, how her sister was missing in action. He had one of his men send her home. She had been in the hospital for a full twenty-four hours. She needed a shower, a bed, and she needed to eat a full meal. There was no way that he would allow her to stress her body any more than she already had.

Of course, she fought him on leaving, but once he put his foot down about it, she obliged. He was lost in his thoughts, thinking about how she was doing at home. All of this stress he knew was too much, especially for a pregnant woman. He slightly rested his head back onto the hospital pillow that was covered in a white case and then stared at the blank wall in front of him. He was pulled from his thoughts when someone entered his room.

"Knock, knock. Someone is up early."

Nova said with a smile as she entered the room. She held a small carton of orange juice in her hand with the straw already sticking out. She closed the door behind her and then stood next to a chair in the room.

"Can I have a seat?" she asked.

Only with him did she display manners that she wouldn't show anywhere else. With anyone else, she was the boss, and she didn't ask shit. Everything that came out of her mouth was an order. Man-Man nodded his head towards the seat. He took in her appearance and noticed that it was a dress down day for her. Since their split, he had never seen her without a heel on her foot or a fur draped on those petite shoulders. In front of him, she was dressed in a Fendi sweatsuit with the matching sneakers. Her natural hair was pulled into a messy bun.

He was glad that she had come because all night he was dying to know how the clean-up job had gone. Messy scenes like the one he was involved in were never his speed, and Nova knew it. Where there were neighbors, there was the possibility of jail time, and that was something that he was never willing to do. Man-Man would have a shoot-out with the police and die in the process before he allowed anyone to chain him up and toss him into a cage like an animal.

"How did it go last night?" he asked, breaking the silence.

From being shot in the neck, his voice was so raspy, and to Nova, it was the sexiest shit ever. It added to his features. Even when he was down, she couldn't deny the qualities he held that made him worthy of being her husband, to begin with. Nova leaned up in the chair to pass him the carton of orange juice. When he grabbed it, she sat back into the chair and crossed one leg over the other. She was so fucking ladylike, yet she held gangsta qualities that most men didn't even possess.

"It was fine. I handled everything. Your television for the room isn't on. If it were, you would have seen that the public is calling it a homicide, suicide."
Man-Man took a sip from the juice and then nodded his head up and down.

"Who is Chad Brewster?" she asked.

Man-Man scrunched his face in thought and then quickly remembered that he had seen the name before. He remembered seeing the same name on paperwork from a pending lawsuit. Chad was a man at his sport's bar that Vincent had broken a bottle over his head a year prior.

"He some nigga that Vincent got into it with at the bar a little minute ago."

Nova shook her head up and down lightly because, over the years, she learned how unpredictable Vincent could have been. He was a walking wild card, which was always a risk, but when it came to business over the years, he had made her and her sister's so much money.

"Well, his body was inside the house. He was badly beaten, tied to a chair and shot."

"Damn... all that?" Man-Man asked.

"Mm-hm, was he getting high again? That can be the only thing that explains all of this."

"He was," Man-Man confirmed.

"Well, the altercation between the two at the bar serves in favor of the story that the news ran with. Now it narrates that Vincent and this Chad guy had some problems brewing, and it ended in bloodshed. That case will be opened and closed."

Man-Man wanted to ask about the neighbors because he was sure that one of them had to hear something. As he was bleeding out on the grass, he vaguely remembered Eternity calling Bleek's name. His real name. If he had heard it, he was sure that a neighbor had to as well. He knew that Nova would have all aspects covered, though, so he didn't dwell on the chance of witnesses. Speaking of cases, he had a couple of questions for her. He cleared his throat, which burned like hell from the damaged tissue.

"What's going on with you?" he asked.

"Oh, the regular, back and forth between here and Egypt. Also, I'm about to—"

"Nova Lee cut the bullshit. Two officers came here for you last night. What's *really* going on with you?" he asked again.

Nova turned in her seat, nervously. She didn't know when her life had become so risky, but now everything was slowly starting to sneak up on her. She was sitting in the hospital room, taking a risk. Her feet on U.S soil could end in turmoil, but she was willing to take these risks for the man that sat in front of her waiting on her to answer.

"What did you say when they came?" she asked.

Man-Man hated when people answered questions with a question, but he could see the uncomfortableness in her glare. The way the creases on her face panned out let him know that she was in some shit, some deep shit.

"I didn't say shit. I was on my way to sleep when they came."

"So then how do you know that they came here for me?" she quickly asked.

"They were talking to my girl."

Nova rolled her eyes. Her annoyance was evident, and she wasn't about to do shit to hide it either. She was sure that Man-Man's new girlfriend probably sailed her ass up the river.

"And no… she didn't say shit. When they asked for *Mrs. Bridges,* she said that she didn't know who that was." Nova sighed with relief once Man-Man stopped speaking.

"I don't know who the fuck that is either. Considering that we are divorced. As to why they are calling you that is beyond me, but we will get to that later. What is going on with you? I know ya ass would never turn rat and twelve only look for people when they ass turn rat or when they wanna take em under. Which one is it?"

Nova looked Man-Man in his eyes and got lost. She always would in those mystery pupils.

"Not here... when you are discharged and healed, we will talk."

Man-Man's eyebrows dipped in anger.

"Nova, I know ya ass did not turn fucking rat!"

"Of course, I didn't!"

She stood from her chair. She was offended, and it showed.

"I would never do that. That will mean telling on you and I will *never* do that to you."

She quickly dressed in her bubble coat before she went to make her exit.

"Text me when you are discharged. We can meet and talk. I've already been here too long." She said quickly before she hurried out of the room.

Uncertainty was weighing heavy on the soul. No amounts of sighs could rid her body of the feeling. She was playing with the thought of really telling her ex-husband what she had done. The reason why she was risking it all every time her feet touched the United States. Nova kicked off of her sneakers and then laid back onto the bed. The hotel room was the presidential suite at one of the most profound hotels in the city. Although she should have been laying low, she preferred to embrace the luxuries that her lifestyle had awarded her with.

She worked hard, damn hard for everything that she currently had. At the time of her starting her operation with her sisters, she was holding down a full-time federal job and pushing drugs. Who the fuck was out here doing that? She knew that she probably should have fled the states and waited for Man-Man to call when he was discharged, but she figured that she would stay put.

Her phone ringing grabbed her attention. When she saw that it was a group video call from her older sisters, she let it ring out. She knew that they would be wondering why she was still in Tennessee. Not wanting to deal with the chastisement from them, she didn't even bother to answer. Her sisters always had her best interest at heart, but she knew that with a situation like this, they wouldn't and couldn't sympathize.

The three of them were all they had, especially after her divorce, so she knew that they wouldn't understand why she wanted to stay until she had that one on one chat with Man-Man. To tell the truth, she was growing tired of the lifestyle that she was living. Everything in her craved the simplicity of life that Man-Man was trying to give her when they were a union.

The home, the white picket fence, dog and the kid, she yearned for that, and so badly she wanted it. She needed it. She didn't know when her head had gone, but she wanted it all back. A little too late, he was now building that with someone else, and she didn't have a home-wrecker bone in her body. If the girl with the baby bump is what was making him happy, then she would have to just respect that. She hated the regret she felt in her heart, though.

So many times during their divorce process, she had asked herself if this is what she had really wanted. Did she want the lifestyle of being a queen pin over the lifestyle that she could have had with her husband? Why couldn't she have it both? Why couldn't she be the boss and have the family behind her? Why couldn't she call the shots, push drugs, and then at the end of a long productive day cuddle in bed with her soulmate?

As another million rolled her way, she turned her back on what Man-Man was trying to offer. If he couldn't get down with her program, then it was fuck him. So many times over the past two years, her mind went back to what had broken them to begin with...

Nova walked around the house with Man-Man on her tail.

"So, you have nothing to say about these shits!" he was yelling.

Which wasn't like him, but the betrayal he felt caused him to. So nonchalantly, Nova moved around the house. She opened the drawer to her nightstand and then pulled her silk scarf out.

After tying it around her head, she finally addressed him. His untamed eyebrows were scrunched in anger. Still, he held the birth control pills in his hand. He had it held up so that she could see what he was holding.

As soon as he started yelling, she already knew that her secret was now out of the bag. She had been caught red-handedly, and she reacted how she usually would have in situations like this. Whenever she was caught up in some shit, she jumped into her nonchalant bag. It didn't matter how extreme the problem was. She put on a front as if she didn't care when, in most cases, she cared deeply. It was the stiff Capricorn in her that kept her steel face on even when she was going through emotional turmoil.

"Marcelo, why are you going through my stuff?"

Taken back by her response, he threw his head back in disbelief. They were two years into their marriage, and now he knew why she hadn't gotten pregnant yet. Where he thought that he was unable to give her children or worse, she wasn't able to reproduce, the standstill in his plans was forced. The key point to their reproduction problems was premeditated. She was taking pills and taking them faithfully to ensure that he couldn't get what he had desperately wanted.

"See now... you got me fucked up for real."

Nova stood on her side of the bed with her arms folded across her breast. If the conversation was of lighter matters, Man-Man would have dicked her down on the bed she stood beside. The same bed where he tried for months to impregnate her. Their bed. She had a thing for wearing silk pajamas to bed, and he loved to see them on her. As he looked at her nonchalant demeanor, it pissed him off further. It was the ugliest he had seen her. That smug facial expression was hurting him to his core. She held no sympathy for her betrayal. He started to grow disgust for the same woman that held his heart. The same woman that was now breaking his heart.

"Why are you taking fucking birth control, Nova?"

"I'm not ready for children. I'm just now seeing a profit from this Heavenz shit. I'm finally getting the money that I want, why would I stop now?"

Man-Man sucked his teeth and then tossed the birth control case onto the bed. He stood at the foot of their king-sized sleigh bed.

"It's not about the money, we had this same conversation last year and what did you say then? You said it was about the money. I have fucking money, and when I have, we have. This is about you not wanting to leave the game alone! Why do you want to stay in that shit? Is it power? Is it the feeling you get when you walk into a room and notice how grown-ass fucking men cower? What the fuck is it huh? What the fuc—"

"YES!"

Finally, she had admitted what he knew in his heart of hearts for the past two years. She had no intention of leaving the game alone. She had no plans on giving him children either, at least not right now. He was a compromising person, and she was showing how stingy she was. How could she pretend for a year to try for a baby? With every month and every pregnancy test that came up negative, she showed genuine disappointment. Could she be that good of an actress? It was a dangerous trait to Man-Man.

She possessed the ability to naturally lie in the face of someone she loved. This made him question her love for him. This made him question her loyalty.

"Yea, we're done here."

He was tired of beating a dead ass horse. She wasn't bending on the topic of leaving the game, and he felt like he was more than patient with her. He gave her a year to shake that street shit, a year to pull it together and become the wifey that he knew she could be, but she had no desire to do any of it.

"What do you mean?" she asked as she watched him quickly pull a pair of jeans over his basketball shorts. He stepped his socked feet into a pair of his sneakers that were at the foot of the bed, and then he started to exit the bedroom.

"Marcelo? Why can't I have both?" she asked.

"If I'm out of that life, why can't you be? Why does my fucking wife want to be Griselda Blanco so fucking bad? Instead of talking to me about the shit, you took birth control for a year. Behind my back at that. How much longer would you have been taking them shits, all while convincing me that we could just try again... huh?"

Nova said nothing because she didn't have an answer for him. She loved the way being boss made her feel. She was a true queen pin, and she carried herself as such. At first, he found it incredibly sexy, but now, all he wanted was for her to carry herself as his wife, and that's it.

"So, you're leaving me?" she asked with a straight face.

Visibly unaffected and unfazed, but inside, she was dying with each inch he took closer to their room door.

"I want my wife to get high off life from being a wife, a mother, a legit business owner, not the fucking plug. So yeah, I'm done here." He said before he walked out of the room...

Nova wiped away a lone tear that cascaded down her face. With her eyes fixated on the ceiling, she thought of all of the time she had wasted chasing the bag. She had millions, but it honestly didn't mean shit, with no one standing at her side to reap the benefits with her.

*C*hapter 6

Bleek stood in front of the full-length body mirror with a saddened expression as he took his suit jacket off. It was seven days later, and still, no one had heard a thing from Eternity. After having the DNA test done in the hospital, it was proven, without a doubt, that Bleek was the late baby Malik's father. That he knew and he didn't even want to bother with the DNA test, but for him to make the proper funeral arrangements, it had to be done. He loosened his tie from around his neck, took it off, and then threw it onto the hotel's bed.

The weight of the world rested on his broad shoulders as he slowly got himself undressed and quickly changed into clothing more comfortable. The funeral service for his son was beautiful. He wanted to cremate his child and then take the ashes with him, but he couldn't be that selfish. He wouldn't be that selfish. Even with all that Eternity had a hand in that put them in this current situation still, he couldn't do that to her.

He hated that he laid his boy to rest in the same state where he was taken from, but in a sense, it was mutual ground. Tori lived there, he had a business there, and Eternity had given life to the baby there. Although she was still in the wind, he wanted it to be easy for her to find him if she ever wanted to visit.

Knock, knock

A gentle knock caught his attention. He slowly walked over to the door to answer it. He had hope that Eternity would show her face. He texted her constantly. After sending her the address of where the funeral would be held and the burial, he also made sure to send the address to the hotel where he was staying. He silently prayed that it was her at the door because there was no need to stay in Chattanooga once the day was done.

Bleek pulled the door open to see Tori standing in front of him. Her eyes were red and puffy from hours of crying. Despite her broken demeanor, her pregnancy had her glowing past her heartache. The black dress she wore hugged her new curves and ended at her calf. Bleek took in her beauty and smiled. He knew that her child would bring her all of the joy that she would need.

He blinked away tears when his thoughts went back to Eternity. He couldn't understand how she could leave everyone, even her sister. He knew that everyone mourned differently, but to him, they should have been all in this together. Didn't Tori have enough on her plate as is? She was pregnant with a boyfriend that was just recently shot, and now, she too was mourning the death of her nephew.

"Are you leaving soon?" She asked weakly when she noticed the packed luggage nearby.
At a time where she felt she should be her happiest, she was miserable.

"Yea."
Bleek opened his arms, and Tori went to hug him.

This was the farewell that she was dreading. With her sister in the wind, she knew that it would be less likely that she would see Bleek anytime soon.

"I'm going to give you my new number when I get it," Bleek said lowly as he gently rubbed Tori's back.
He felt her back heaving up and down, so he knew that she was crying.

"You're changing your number?"
Tori broke their embrace as she asked in shock.

"I have to... she didn't even come to the funeral. I just need to break away."

Bleek used his thumb to flick his nose and sniffle when his orbs held a mist over them.

This emotional side of him was still so new. He thought that he was emotionally spent when he was doing the back and forth thing with Eternity, but this, the loss of his son, had definitely taken the cake. Randomly throughout the day, his emotions hit him. He couldn't understand how he missed something so much that he never got the chance to experience. Maybe he was mourning the opportunity that was abruptly taken away from him. He envisioned himself changing diapers. He pictured the phases that his son was supposed to go through. Learning to crawl and then walk.

Bleek would do anything to see that robotic two-step that all babies did when they were first finding their footing. That wobble would bring him so much joy. His eyes watered just thinking about it. Just thinking about the what-ifs brought so much pain to his soul.

"You didn't hear me?"

Bleek blinked his eyes twice to pull himself together, and then he gave his attention to Tori.

"I'm sorry sis. Na, I didn't hear you."

Tori studied him. She saw the pain in his eyes, the same exact pain that her sister held in her eyes the night they discovered that baby Malik was missing. She cleared her throat before she spoke.

"Are you leaving today?"

"Yes."

Bleek didn't waste any time answering the question. He was needed back home. Besides his mechanical shop needing his attention, he needed to breathe, and he couldn't do that in Chattanooga.

"Okay," Tori sighed, "let me let you go." She smiled weakly.

As Tori started to walk out of the room, Bleek called out to her.

"Yo, Tori."

She turned around to give him her full attention.

"Take care of yourself."

Tori tilted her head to the side as she registered everything. She felt like this would be her last time seeing him.

"You too," she said in a low tone just before she made her exit.

Bleek sighed and then looked over at his packed luggage. The back of his hand itched like hell from the healing phase of his new artwork. After patting the spot aggressively to rid himself of the itch, a chill came over his body, and then he quickly shook it off. *Where the fuck are you, E?* He thought to himself. He breathed deeply and then grabbed the handle to his luggage. While walking out of his room, he walked straight into Sha.

"You ready to go bro?"

Bleek looked Sha up and down before he responded. He was thankful for his boy. From the day at the hospital, he had never left his side.

"Yea, it's time to go the fuck home."

Bleek said as he slowly closed the room door behind him.

Chapter 7

Eternity laid on the cold grass with a throw blanket covering her body. The bitter sting from the January's air did nothing to her skin. She was cold and numb from the inside to the out. As tears filled her orbs and then cascaded down her cold chubby cheeks, she gathered the fresh dirt beneath her into the palm of her hand. She felt closer to her baby as she laid across his grave. Her cellphone beside her vibrated, and she didn't even bother to open her eyes to check and see who it was.

She figured that it was either Tori or Bleek, and if it weren't them, then it was somebody, an associate or old coworker wishing her a happy birthday. On her day, she just wanted to spend the moment with one person, with her son. So much that she had hopped the graveyard's gate just to spend time with her boy. With an injured foot and all, she scaled the gate to feel something, to feel anything because lately, her days had been empty.

She didn't regret not attending his funeral because she knew that she couldn't withstand it. She hated putting everything onto Bleek's shoulders, but she knew that he could handle it. He was a stronger person than she was. If she would have been present at her son's funeral, then she would have had to go into the ground because there was no way that she could watch them lower that tiny casket into the dirt. She couldn't believe that she had witnessed her son's first breath and also his last. A piece of her would forever be in the ground six feet beneath her.

Snot ran from her nose due to her tears and also the frigid temperature outside. She needed her space after her son's death. The peace of mind that space would grant her was required. So, she took that. She was taking that. She watched his ceremony and burial from a distance because up close would have been too much. It was beautiful, oh so beautiful and she knew that it would be. She knew that Bleek would make sure of it. There was no way that a piece of him was getting sent off any other way besides the best way. Her balled fist went up to her chest as she wept. She didn't care that she was getting moist dirt onto the front of her beige coat.

It was like she had to check her own pulse to make sure that she wasn't going into shock. Her breathing was too erratic and unstable. It felt like her heartbeat had quickened. *Breathe...* Suddenly, Bleek's voice played in her head. His tone always leveled her. He always kept her grounded. She exhaled as she heard his voice in her head again. *Breathe...*

Slowly, her breathing stabilized. She sat onto her butt and then draped the blanket around her shoulders. She knew that she didn't have much time until the groundskeeper did his rounds. Every night since the burial, she had spent two hours with her boy. That's how much time it took the guard to cover the grounds. Two hours out of her day were the best hours because she felt closer to her son.

On this night, she was saying goodbye. Chattanooga held so much heartbreak in her. What was supposed to be a fresh start quickly turned to tragic memories? She remembered when Bleek had told her that the city was suffocating to him, and now she knew first-hand how that felt. She tilted her head to the side and then ran two fingers across her son's tombstone. She smiled at the engraved name on the marble. Malik Renmen Washington-Browne.

Without approval, Bleek had added his name to that tombstone. Even if it was frowned upon since the attending guest that wasn't immediate family at the service didn't know him as the father, he didn't give a fuck. His DNA was beneath her feet, and she knew that he would always associate himself with her child, with their child. She kissed her two cold fingertips and then gently pressed it against the marble tombstone.

"Mommy has to go so bye, my baby. I love you so much, baby boy. I love you so much, my love."

Eternity lifted her coat sleeve and then kissed the fresh tattoo on her inner wrist that read *Renmen* in script lettering. It was so small and dainty, but it stood out because her body was ink-free prior. That one word that one name meant so much to her. *Love* in the Haitian language because her baby was made with love. She gave props to the twenty-five percent of Bleek that he swept under the rug constantly. Eternity loved everything about that man, and that included his roots. She loved all of the parts of him that he didn't even love himself.

He didn't speak on his roots, but she was well vested in the knowledge of that man. She knew about everything that had made him the man he was. When she stood to her feet, light snow started to fall from the sky. She took the blanket off of her shoulders and then dressed his space. She had just gotten up from the soil, so she knew that it was cold. Her natural body heat no longer covered the space beneath her. She couldn't leave her baby like that.

Once she was satisfied with the placement of the blanket over her baby's grave, she made her exit. It took her no time to climb over the same gate she straddled to get in. Parked on the outskirts of the graveyard was a car that she had rented. She sat into the car and gathered herself before she pulled off.

She drove to a nearby motel. This day would be her last one in the city, she needed a fresh start. She was sick and tired of running to Bleek whenever she was in turmoil. Why should he always and only see her when she was at her worst point? She knew that she needed to get her together. The next time that she stepped into his presence, she wanted to be whole. She was so over being the glued together girl that he had grown to love.

He was infatuated with the tiny glued together pieces called Eternity. She was fragile, so fragile, and when her life did the Humpty Dumpty, and she fell off that wall, he was on standby with superglue. She couldn't and wouldn't allow that to happen anymore.

When she made it to her motel, she parked right in front of her room and then quickly went inside. She flicked on the lights and then cringed at the place. This is where she had been held up since her son had died. The space surrounding her was well below her standards. Bleek had given her nothing but the best, and then behind him, Vincent tried his best to keep up with her spoiled materialistic ways, but she knew that it didn't matter how much he had gifted her with, his bag was nothing compared to Bleek's.

Eternity pulled her two suitcases to the front door. Briefly, she remembered when she had ransacked her home to get some of her belongings. She knew that Tori and Bleek would be too busy with funeral arrangements to scourer the streets for her. It was the perfect time to get her shit and break away. She reached under the desk in the room and picked up her duffle bag.

After sitting it on the empty other queen-sized bed in the room that was currently being used as storage, she unzipped the bag to make sure that the contents were still inside of it. Stacks of money peered up at her. The day after her son had died, she cleared all of her accounts. The day after that, the life insurance policy that she had on Vincent was ready to be paid out. She stood in the dingy hotel room fifty thousand dollars richer.

While with him, she didn't pray on his downfall, but after she had fled the state the first time and made it up in her mind that she would give him a second chance, she needed that extra insurance. She thought that she would be the one to end him and then find a way to cover it up if he would have put hands on her again, but life worked out differently. She felt absolutely nothing with his passing. In her mind, she hated that he had died so quickly. Yes, she blamed herself for what had happened to her son, but she pointed a finger his way as well.

When everything had hit the fan, she knew then that the love that Vincent had for her child was false. If it were real, truly real, there was no way that he would have allowed any harm to come to her son's way. For the entire day that her son was missing with Vincent, she begged God to make it possible for her to trade places with her child. She would have given her life to save him. She sighed as she zipped the duffle bag closed. Just thinking about the situation set fire to her skin.

"Ughhh!" she groaned as she turned on her heels and then made her way to the nearby bathroom.

She clicked on the light upon entering the room, and the illumination flickered. Once the flickering stopped, she looked at her reflection in the mirror. The bags under her eyes were a reminder that it had been a while since she had last slept. She ran her open hand over her neck and lightly massaged the tension out of her muscles or attempted to.

There was nothing that she could do to ease her body of that tension. She knew that with the loss of her son that the feeling was permanent. She picked up the pendant to the necklace that she was wearing. The small gold baby feet locket rested on the inside of her fingers. Sealed inside was a piece of her son's umbilical cord. The article was custom made, and she had waited all of these days in Chattanooga for it.

Bleek had taught her long ago that any jewelry that graced her body should be custom made because she was one of a kind. She wasn't like any other bitch around her, so she shouldn't have to get anything that anyone else had. She picked the pendant up and then gently kissed it. She tilted her head to the side as she observed her matted hair in the mirror. Her phone vibrating in her back pocket made her stop observing herself briefly.

Malik

"Happy birthday, E. Stop forcing yourself to be alone. You need to grieve, and you need to grieve properly. We can do it together. Shed tears with me, ma. Get through this WITH me."

Eternity's floodgates opened as she read the text. Bleek's standard texts would all be messages of him demanding to know where she was. This message was thoughtful, and she didn't know if it was the new year, but she was so close to responding. She pulled her bottom lip, in-between her teeth, to stop it from shaking. She blew out a sharp breath before she mumbled under her breath.

"You can't keep trying to fix me. Let me fix me. Let me finally come back to you whole," she whispered.

She spoke as if someone was inside of the small, dimly lit bathroom with her. She was tired of being this man's science project. She knew her soul was damaged; it always had been, and ever since she had met him, he tried to make it his business to mend it. It wasn't his job to do, though. She knew that she always knew that, but still, she allowed his attempts at fixing her.

For years she thought that it was his duty to do so. As unfortunate as it was, it took for the loss of her child to see that him fixing her was impossible. All of the broken bits in her body had to be fixed by her and her only. She gave her attention back to her hair and then groaned. Saying goodbye to Chattanooga meant saying goodbye to Chavella too. She looked at the scissors that were placed onto the bathroom sink, and then she picked them up. She snipped away at her hair.

As pieces of her tresses fell down her shoulders and then hit, the floor weight started to lift from her. She went snip happy, and by the time she was done, her hair was a small afro. She tossed the scissors onto the counter and then squealed.

"Oh, my fucking Goddddd…" she put her hands over her mouth, "I look like fucking Maya Angelou."
She hissed under her fingertips.

After dropping her hands to her side, she rolled her neck around and pouted. It felt oh so good to snip that hair, but suddenly she regretted it.

"Ughh," she groaned.

She quickly exited the bathroom and then dug around in one of her bags for a headscarf. She ended up pulling out a bonnet, so she tossed that on her head instead. After packing up her rental with her luggage, she eased out of her park to drive around to the lobby to give her hotel key back. Once she was back in her car, she hit the road. The only place she thought of going was to her aunt's house in Georgia. The same aunt that had housed Tori while she was locked up.

She knew that it was late, but she figured that her aunt would be up because of the holiday. On the second ring, a groggy voice answered.

"Hello?"

"Auntie Nora?" Eternity said with question.

"Eternity?"

Eternity sighed in relief. The last she had spoken to her aunt was when she had first moved down to Tennessee.

"Hey, auntie..."

"Girl, if you coming... come on."

Eternity scrunched her face in confusion. She knew that her aunt was always good at reading people, but she knew that she wasn't this good. Before she could even think any further, her aunt cleared her thoughts.

"Tori called me a few days ago asking if you were here or if I had spoken to you. I'm so sorry about what happened, baby. Come on and bring ya behind out here. I'll text you the address. Come heal your soul, baby. I won't tell no one that you're here until it's time for me to."

Eternity's eyes watered as her heart smiled. She had missed her aunt. Her soul was so pure, but her mouth wasn't. She didn't take any shit. She knew that more than anyone that her aunt could sympathize with her pain. Auntie Nora only had one child, a girl, and when her daughter was seven, she died from drowning at the public pool.

Auntie Nora had taken her eyes off of Tori and her daughter for one split second. Eternity remembered the day oh so well. She wasn't there because she was locked up, but Tori had explained the day in such great detail that she felt like she was there.

"Thank you, Auntie Nora," Eternity's voice cracked. *"Drive safely."*

Once the line was ended soon after Eternity felt her phone vibrate in the cupholder. She reached down to get her phone. Quickly she put the address that her aunt had sent her into the GPS on her phone. *Lilburn?* She thought to herself. She figured that all black people that relocated from New York to Georgia moved straight to Atlanta, but she could see that by the address her aunt had sent that Nora opted for another part of the state. Eternity was grateful that the drive was only two hours because she was growing tired. She knew that she could do a two-hour drive like it was nothing. She cracked her window, turned the radio up, and then put mashed her foot on the gas.

𝒞hapter 8

Bleek drug his feet across the polished concrete floors of the lobby to his building.

"Welcome back from your trip Mr. Browne."

"Thanks, Alexander," Bleek said to the doorman that stood guard in the lobby.

"Mr. Brown so there's a —"

Bleek held his hand up as he strolled past. He was exhausted for the night, and he didn't have it in him to discuss what he was sure would be something about a package that came in his mail.

"Please, Alexander. Not today. Just not today. Tomorrow say to me whatever it is that you were just going to."

Bleek didn't even wait for the man to respond. He kept walking towards the elevators that were located in the back of the lobby.

When the steel box descended to his level, he stepped inside. During the ride to the top, he thought about his plane ride. He thought about why he had been gone for almost nine days, the baby he put to rest invaded his thoughts. When he discovered his son's middle name, he loved Eternity even more. He was pissed that his son had her last name. He was grateful that Malik didn't have Vincent's last name, but still, his surname was the one that should have been on his son's birth certificate. Since it wasn't done, he damn sure had it placed on the tombstone above his resting grounds.

The bell dinged, indicating that he had reached his floor. When he stepped off of the elevator, he was faced with Paris. She sat on the floor next to his front door. The toes of her Balenciaga sneakers touched one another, her back curved over like a turtle's shell, and her arms were placed onto both of her lifted knees. She didn't even notice that he was approaching her. He knew that it was her, though. The way the denim jeans she wore hugged her curves always pulled the same reaction out of him. He smelled her signature scent that came in a bottle from Valentino. She was provided with nothing but the best from young, and it showed. Even with being so grown, she would give herself nothing short of it.

Although her entire outfit was thrown on, it was expensive and fashionable. She always made sure to be at her best, and Bleek liked that about her. It was clear that she had fallen asleep while trying to wait for him. He had been gone for days, and he wondered how many of them did she do precisely this. He knew that Alexander probably let her up without informing him because he was so used to seeing the pair together. He probably figured that she had a key.

As Bleek looked down at her, he had half a mind to leave her there. He tapped the pockets of his sweats and felt for his keys. He took them out carefully and then with his free hand, he silently picked up his suitcase by the handle. He stepped around her. Slowly he pulled the key that he needed from the ring and tried to put it into the door. When the keys hit the floor beside her, she quickly lifted her head from her knees and looked up at him. *Not today, please...* he thought.

Since the day he had lost his son every day after it was a *not today* kind of day. His patience was none, and his feelings were nonexistent. He didn't need the dose of Paris that he knew she was about to give. He didn't need that dose of drama. *Not today.* When they locked eyes, she slowly stood to her feet. Her jacket was draped around her forearm, and her Celine purse hung from the other. She stood in front of him, looking like a slice of perfection, but he wouldn't indulge, he couldn't. *Just not today.* He thought about his unmanageable emotions. He had been all over the place, so over the place and he hated it.

"You were going to go inside and leave me out here?"

He heard the hurt in her voice, and at that moment, he regretted the decision that he was about to make. But God, he just needed a moment of peace. He just needed a moment to himself. He was going through hardships that he knew she wouldn't understand. It had nothing to do with the fact that she wasn't a parent because, in his eyes, he was never one either, but it wasn't by choice. He knew that she wouldn't understand because what he was battling was part of his life that he loved to keep locked away.

Eternity was the part of him that he was selfish with, he guarded anything that had to do with her. That was the protector instincts in him. The same protection he cloaked Eternity in would have been the same blanket of security that he would have draped around his son, had he known. Just thinking about it took all the minimal energy that he had left.

"Just not today Paris." He said lowly as he quickly picked up his house keys and then turned the one he needed into the door.

He quickly walked over the threshold, pulling his suitcase behind him. It made no sense to carry it when what he was trying to avoid was happening anyway.

"Listen…" she walked in the door behind him. Bleek threw his head back and then sighed dramatically. He wanted her to just leave. If he had to show his asshole side, then so be it. The subtle hints that he was giving that said he just needed time to himself, at least today, wasn't enough for her. He knew damn well that she wasn't blind to it.

Paris Shaw didn't let anything go undetected. Like her father, the Florida state attorney general, she was so observant that nothing went under her radar without her peeping game first. She noticed the new ink on his hand when he turned his key in the door before they had walked in. *Renmen.* Unfamiliar with the meaning of the word, she could only conclude that the name belonged to a woman. She was tired of concluding, though, she was tired of assuming. Bleek hadn't given her any reason to believe that he would dog her so she wouldn't treat him like it.

"You said listen... go. Speak ya peace before it's time for you to go."

Bleek's tone was harsh. It was so unfamiliar. He had been stern with her in the past, but never had he been harsh. The most upset she had seen him was when she had pried into the relationship between him and Toya. That sternness made her nervous. What he was projecting now was fucking with her, but she had those big girl undies on. She wasn't going to run because she felt that he was obviously trying to push her away.

"I was worried about you every single day that you were gone. I don't know what happened, but I can sense that you haven't spoken about whatever it is. You're not the same from when you left, something is missing. A little piece of your heart is gone. Let someone in so that you can talk. It seems like you need to vent. I can see in the way your shoulders are hanging, there is a lot on them. I know what you're carrying is heavy, so let me carry some of it for you."

She was standing in front of him, begging him for the same exact shit that he was asking Eternity for, a way in. She wanted him to open up to her the same way he wanted Eternity to open up to him.

"You should go."

"No," she quickly said.

Bleek raised his eyebrow and then let go of the handle to his suitcase.

"Paris don't make me put you on the other side of my door."

Paris planted her feet and then tried to hold her weight down.

In the past, she complained about the extra weight that she carried around, but Bleek never had a problem swooping her frame into his strong arms with ease. If he could lift all 230 pounds of her during pleasure, she should have known that he could do it at the moment.

"I'm not going anywhere, Malik. You need to let someone in. If you don't want this anymore, that's fine, but still, you *need* someone to let your shit out on. Let me be that person."

Bleek sighed as he cupped his face with his hands.

"Paris... get out."

He just needed this one day to get his shit straight. He was a bottler, a builder. He would lay his emotions down in the form of bricks and build a house before he vented. Fuck that, he would make a six-floor apartment building before he vented. He never had anyone to vent to, and with almost thirty years on earth, he didn't need one now.

Although Ty was a listening ear, he preferred to keep his battles to himself. Hell, his friend had enough struggles that he had to fight on his own.

"No," her voice sounded small.

He dropped his hands from his face and made eye contact with her. A light mist laid over her brown almond-shaped orbs. It was an indication that tears were on the horizon.

"I just need today to put my shit back in place. Get the fuck out!" Bleek growled.

"No!"

Bleek hemmed up Paris by the arm and then started to walk her to his door.

"I'm not going to leave you! It's all over your face Malik. How many people have left you in life? I won't be one of them. Let me in." She said everything in one breath as she struggled with him pushing her out.

Bleek closed his eyes tightly as he held onto her.

"Did Renmen leave you?" she asked.

Bleek tightened his grip on her shirt.

"Don't say his fucking name. Don't ever let that name leave your fucking lips."

"His?" Paris questioned.

She quickly thought of the tattoo on his chest that read his mother's name. She didn't know the full story of the woman that had birthed the man in front of her, but she knew that she was no longer here.

She didn't know of Bleek's street ways, but she knew he had some street in him. A hood nigga with a business. One that had polished himself up to look good for society, but still, he was a hood nigga, nonetheless. Those hood dudes treated their bodies as a canvas when they lost a loved one. Paris wondered who Renmen could have been, but at the moment, it didn't even matter. The pain that was etched across Bleek's face told her that he needed someone, he needed her.

The lines of stress that were imprinted across his forehead told a story that she needed to know, but she wouldn't push him for it just yet.

"You need to fucking go."
Bleek continued to usher her to the door. When he got to the front door, he swung it open with his free hand.

"You need love, Malik. When you were gone, I realized that I love you. I love you soooo much, and right now, you need love. You need someone to love you to fill this void. Let me fill that void."
Bleek broke.

"No one can fill that void. No one—" his voice cracked, *"nobody* can make this shit better." He said barely above a whisper.

He had her hemmed up against the open front door.

"I don't need anybody to love me, Paris. I'm not worth loving. If you were smart, you would walk out that door and not come back. Bad shit happens around me. Bad shit happens to me. Who the fuck wants that for their life?" Bleek choked out as tears danced down his face. He thought about the love he yearned for throughout his life.

He begged for love from his mother. His grandmother ended up giving it to him naturally, but after she died, he had that part of him yearning for love once more. From her, it jumped to Eternity. He thought about what he was responsible for, the death of his own child. In his lifestyle, he had only regretted taking life only once before then.

Since that day, he moved smarter. He moved more strategically. The day he shot his son played in his head over and over. He thought of ways he would have moved differently in the situation, and he couldn't come up with anything.

Not going into the house was not an option for him. He was sure that he had done everything right. He was convinced that he had dotted his I's and crossed his T's. If that was the case, he wondered how things could have ended so tragically.

"But you are worth loving. You taught me so much. I can't help but love you."
Bleek rested his forehead to hers. With the door to his condo wide open, they stood against it, forehead to forehead. She breathed heavily from the scuffle of Bleek trying to get her out, they were both breathing heavily.

"Loving me is going to hurt you." He admitted.

"Let me worry about my hurt." She pulled her bottom lip, in-between her white teeth.

She was nervous. So nervous. She didn't expect Bleek to reveal his love for her because she wasn't sure if there was any there. She said what she said, and she had to get the shit off her chest. Paris envisioned that the first time she used the four-letter word would be on better terms. Perhaps over dinner or a date night inside, but she was going to take what she could get.

Bleek finally let go of the shoulder of her shirt, and then he backed away to give her the space that was needed. She reached her hand up and then wiped the trail of tears that stained his chocolate skin. She cupped his face as she spoke.

"You are so worth loving Malik. Your heart is golden, anybody in your life that can't or refuses to see that shit doesn't deserve to be in your life."

She was speaking confidence and love into him, like how a mother would. Like how he wished that his mother would have done years ago when he was a young boy. Like how his grandmother used to before the grim reaper took her away. Like how Eternity would.

He whimpered in her hand. Finally, he was releasing all of the backed-up hurt. She stood there and held him as he let it all out. As the robust frame stood in her doting arms, she lightly caressed his firm back. She had the warm aura, and Bleek could tell that it was rooted in her because of her upbringing.

"Shh, shh," she hushed as she slowly walked backward, still with him in her arms so that she could close the front door.

"Every fucking body leaves. My mother, my brother moved to a whole different country. *Her. She* left me and now my boy. My fucking boy."

Paris knew that the *her* he was talking about had to be another woman. She just assumed that the boy he was speaking of was a friend. The man that was holding onto her as he wept was so weak. She had never seen him this way.

"Breathe…" she coached.

The same word he used hundreds of times to calm Eternity was now getting used on him. The irony. Bleek exhaled in skips as he still cried. He looked Paris in her eyes and saw the good in her. He saw the sympathy in her glare.

The Malik she always laid eyes on was usually stoic. He was serious, always serious, and he came across as emotionless. As floods escaped from the windows to his soul, she then knew that he felt. He felt so much. He carried so much on his shoulders. So, he didn't rush his grieving process. Without knowing the specifics, she would be there for him. She made the vow to herself. Seeing him so broken, she knew that he needed somebody in his corner. So, she waited patiently for all of the pain to leave his body.

When he had finally calmed down, she had led him to his bathroom. She ran a shower for him and then undressed him. His solid frame was artwork to her. As she peeled the clothes off of him, her garden whispered to her to take it there, but she knew that she couldn't. She opened the glass door for him and watched as he stepped inside. He stood under the two shower heads with his dome bowed. She could tell that he was controlling his breathing by the way his back heaved up and down. Slowly, the muscles in-between his shoulder blades flexed1 with each breath.

When him showering was done, she handed him his towel so that he could dry off and then his robe that was always placed on the back of the bathroom door. Countless times she wrapped herself in the cotton material after a warm shower. The robe wrapped around her frame had always hugged her curves. On his body, the material hugged muscle. He was sculpted perfectly. He kept up with his body, and it showed.

Paris watched as his shoulder blades involuntarily flexed as he put the robe on. Dick hanging in between those toned thighs looked like art. *Oh Lord, please let him cover-up and do it quickly.* Paris thought as her loins started to warm up. She observed his face, really observed his face, and saw the bags under his pupils. She wondered what the days away from her had done to him. She wanted him to reveal everything to her in his own time, but the curiosity was killing her. She pushed the urge to know into the back of her mind and brought the need and want to care for him in this time of tragedy to the forefront.

He walked out of the bathroom with his shoulders hung low to anyone who hadn't witnessed him breaking down just moments before it would appear as if he was mopping. The brokenness in his heart caused those shoulders to fall, though. He crawled into his bed.

"Come here."

His tone was even as he requested her presence beside him. She quickly came out of her sneakers and then laid beside him.

"Come out of everything. I need that skin to skin shit." Bleek said, and then he closed his eyes.

He felt the pressure rise from the bed, so he knew that she had gotten up to fulfill his request. When the pressure was applied back to the bed shortly after, he felt her warm body in his arms. He undid the tie to his robe and then opened it up so that he could spoon her.

She turned around and backed that ass up until she felt his warm solid body on her backside. He leaned towards the foot of the bed and then tossed the throw blanket over their bodies.

"Ughhh, the light is still on," Paris groaned. Bleek extended his arms outward and then clapped his hands twice. As soon as he did, the lights shut off.

"Wait a minuteeee. I've been here numerous times, and I never knew you had those clap on clap off ass lights."

"You learn something new every day." He said casually.

"So… how come when you be busting my ass in here, they don't flick on and off. Cause all this junk in my truck damn sure be clapping."

Bleek laughed so hard. Without opening his eyes, he exploded into laughter. She laughed along with him. She didn't know that she had just made his night.

"I needed that," Bleek sighed, "I love your sense of humor Ms. Shaw."

"And I love you…"

She didn't care how many times she had to openly say it until the feeling was reciprocated. She would shout it from the tallest building in Miami. He kissed the nape of her neck and then snuggled into her more. Bleek was a man that moved on his own time, so he didn't have a response for her. He held her tightly as he fell asleep.

$\mathcal{C}$hapter 9

Eternity rushed out of her car and ran into the arms of her aunt. It was refreshing, so refreshing to be in the arms of a loved one.

"Okay, baby, I know…" her aunt's words were soothing.

Eternity broke in her caring arms. Auntie Nora had always given the girls motherly love, especially since her younger sister, Eternity's, and Tori's mother's demons prevented her from doing so. Nora broke their embrace and then cupped Eternity's chin.

"I got you baby. Ya hear me? I got you."

Nora looked in her niece's eyes and saw the hurt in them. The damage was so familiar, oh so familiar. Just when she was around Eternity's age. She was broken. A piece of her would always be missing. A part of her died when her daughter did, so she knew that Eternity carried around that same pain. The pain felt so heavy, so suffocating all of the time.

"Come on, let's get out of this cold. My robe ain't equipped for this shit." Nora said with a soft smile and sass. Eternity smiled and then went back to her car to get her suitcase and duffle bag.

She watched her aunt climb a flight of stairs that led to her apartment. The complex that Nora lived in was a quiet one or at least seemed quiet from what Eternity could see at first glance. After locking up the rental that she had to return the next day, she walked up the flight of stairs and then pushed open the slightly open door.

"Shoes off at the door," she heard Nora call out from somewhere in the back of the apartment.

Eternity smiled. Nora still had that OCD heavy. It was that same trait in her that had whipped Tori's ass into shape. While Eternity was behind bars on a penitentiary schedule, Tori was on the outside with drill sergeant Nora.

Nora peeked her head from around a wall. After taking off her Ugg boots and leaving them at the door, Eternity walked through the open concept living room and walked through the dining room to meet her aunt that was standing in the kitchen.

"Your bathroom and your bedroom is right there." Nora pointed to the right of them. "Over there," she pointed to the left of them, "is my bedroom and bathroom."

Eternity smiled. The apartment was a nice size and perfect for Nora. Actually, it was a little too much space for her.

"Just you moved out here, auntie, and you got a two-bedroom. You could have gotten you a little one-bedroom loft or something."

"I was so used to having a two-bedroom ever since I had your cousin. It doesn't matter where I move. Shit, I could pick up and go to Alaska you better believe I'ma demand that my igloo have a second bedroom. It's just nice to feel her in spirit, you know."

Eternity listened intently as she picked up her necklace from her neck and then kissed the pendant. She would never take it off because it gave her strength. It was a constant reminder for her to get her shit together because she had a guardian angel looking down on her that she couldn't disappoint. So badly she wanted to end it all just to get a chance to see his face again. That small chocolate face and that gum filled smile. She would do anything to see those deep dimples form on those chubby baby cheeks. She would do anything to hear him laugh—just one more time.

What halted her from carrying out her deed was that she was sure that if she ended her life that she wouldn't see her beautiful baby boy at all. She was convinced that when she took her last breath that her soul would get sent straight to hell. She had taken a life, physically killed a man, and she felt responsible for the death of her son. Two bodies stained her resume, and she just knew that those bodies were the signature on the permission slip that would send her straight to hell. Besides her fear of a cruel afterlife, she couldn't leave Tori and Bleek behind. She had already been so selfish, and her ending her own life would be more selfish shit on top of the other selfish shit that she had done to them.

She picked up and left without even letting either one of them know that she was alright, but she just needed space. She needed to breathe. The entire situation took the breath from her body. Every second that passed, she just wanted to scream, she wanted to break shit, and she wanted to explode, a fucking walking time bomb. She was an unpredictable mess, so she distanced herself.

To end the eerie silence that lingered between the two women, Nora spoke again.

"Gone head and get in that room and get you some rest. I'ma try and take you down to my job tomorrow to get you in."

"Job?" Eternity asked with a raised eyebrow.

"Yessss JOB Eternity. I know ya ass don't need the cash you got clothes tossed on, and still, I see the price in the labels, but you need to stay busy. Working a job is a good distraction. Gone head and git."

Eternity chuckled at how her aunt had grown a little southern twang in her accent.

"Goodnight, Auntie, Nora."

"Night, baby."

Eternity walked into the bedroom that was now temporarily hers and then closed the door behind her. The room's décor was simple, a standard queen size bed, two nightstands, and a dresser with a television on top. It was the simplicity of the room that warmed Eternity's heart. The familiarity that her aunt brought her felt amazing. She came out of her clothes. Just panties, bra, and bonnet remained.

After tucking her body under the covers, she just laid there. She just wanted to lay in her sorrow. The pillow beneath her started to soak in her tears. She practiced her breathing. *1, 2, 3, 4, 5... 5, 4, 3, 2, 1...* It didn't matter if she counted up or down. The end result was still the same. Her emotions were still a rollercoaster.

She pinched the bridge of her nose, and when that did nothing, she sucked her teeth. Why didn't it work? Why couldn't she control her demeanor? Why couldn't she stabilize her emotions? She gasped, and it sounded of pain. The bed she laid in lightly shook because of her sobs. She heard the door open, and then she felt pressure on the bed behind her.

"Shh... shh..." Nora rubbed Eternity's shoulder lovingly as she spooned her.

Eternity closed her eyes and welcomed her aunt's embrace. She needed it. God, she wanted the arms that were wrapped around her to belong to one person. To belong to Bleek, but she wouldn't allow him to piece her together anymore. She couldn't. She had to ride this storm out on her own. She knew that when she came out on the other side of it that she would be so beautiful.

She would be that rainbow after the storm that movies and books spoke of. She never saw a rainbow because in her life the storm never ended. *This shit ends now,* she thought as she closed her eyes tightly and sobbed. She sobbed until she couldn't anymore. When no more tears fell from her eyes, her body still shook to force them out. Soon, she was sleep.

Chapter 10

Eternity woke to the smell of breakfast, which was the norm in Nora's household. She didn't care how early a task had to be done eating breakfast was vital to her. Nora would say that breakfast was the most important meal of the day. Eternity rolled over and saw that a plate was rested on her nightstand. She felt like she hadn't eaten in days. Besides replenishing her body with liquids, it was like she hadn't consumed food. Anything that she did try to eat only came up. Her stomach was unsettled right along with her soul.

Mentally she was punishing herself in a sense. Why should she be able to enjoy the simple luxuries of eating when her child could no longer. She saw the slight weight loss, and she hated it, but there was nothing that she could do about it. The grits, turkey bacon, eggs, and toast looked so welcoming. The toast was even cut into triangles. Eternity smiled because she remembered when she was a young girl that she used to beg Nora to cut her food that way. She wanted *little boats,* and Nora being the one to spoil the kids, gave her just that.

Things with Eternity's family back then was so good until it wasn't. When her father died, everything went to the shitter. Eternity hated how her mother, Machina, and Nora had fallen out. Nora still begged to see the girls, but Machina was not having it. Eternity didn't know that the ladies falling out with one another had everything to do with her mother's drug habit. Nora didn't dabble in what she called the devil's playground. She smoked her cigarettes and kept to herself.

Before Eternity had ever known of her mother's problem, she would always hear Nora refer to *nose candy and the candy man.* Eternity chalked the candy man up to be the store clerk in the neighborhood's bodega that everyone referred to as Papi. She used to always get candy beaded bracelets for her and Tori from the store. She remembered when she used to get the beaded candy from the store and pretend like she was partaking in the act of indulging in *nose candy.*

She recalled the day so vividly. She put the candy bracelet on her upper lip and then curled her mouth up to her nose to keep the bracelet in place. *This has to be nose candy,* she thought as a child. She caught a whipping from Nora in the middle of her pretending. *"Come on, ToriTee, you bite a candy from your bracelet, put the bracelet on your nose, and then make ya eyes crazy like this. That's what auntie Nora says. She says that nose candy makes mommy crazy."* She remembered that being the last thing, she said before she took a bite of the candy, placed it under her tiny nose, and then rolled her eyes into the back of her head.

A leather belt met the tail of her body before she could even continue her play session. *"Stay ya ass outta grown folk business,"* Nora shouted with each thrash. At that age, she had no idea. Eternity was blind to her mother's addiction. She found out later, though, and in the most gruesome way. Eternity shook the distant memory from her cognitive as she enjoyed the meal. Finally, she had something that she could hold down.

Knock, Knock

"Come in," Eternity called out as she used the paper towel in her hand to wipe the sides of her mouth.

Nora stepped into the room. Her bobbed wig was twisted, as usual. Nora had been wearing wigs all of Eternity's life. She just knew that Nora's real hair had to be down her back, but she was sure that she would never know.

"Come on and get yaself together. I work the night shift, and if you get this job, you will too. Throw on anything, human resources ain't strict with the clothing policy."

"Ughhh," Eternity groaned. She really didn't want to go back to work, but she knew that it wasn't up for debate. She had half a mind to go and get her own apartment just so she didn't have to, but she knew that she needed Nora. The presence of her made Eternity feel like it was okay to live after losing a child. She knew that her aunt had the secret formula to living life after such loss, so anything that Nora suggested, she was willing to do.

"Okay, I'm getting up. Auntie fix ya wig."

Eternity was tired of looking at Nora's side part that was supposed to be a center part.

"Don't worry about my goddamn hair. Ya little shower cap thingy fell off in your sleep. You over there looking like Don muthafucking King, but you worried about my look. Girl, bye."

Nora chuckled before she closed the door behind her when she exited.

Eternity leaped up from the bed and then looked in the mirror that stood on top of the long dresser in the room. She rolled her eyes at the state of her hair. She had forgotten that the night before, she had butchered her shit. She ran her fingers through the mess on top of her head and then sighed. A quick wash and go would have to do for the day. She made a mental note to visit a beautician sometime later that day. It would have to be after she returned the rental and then went to a dealership to get a new car, but it had to be done.

Eternity's tight coils shrunk in size, but the leave-in conditioner she applied gave her tresses a curly look. She had already returned her rental and was now riding in Nora's car with her.

"You sure you want to dish out money on a car right now? Me and you can make this one car thing work, especially if we're going to be at the same job." Nora suggested as she maneuvered on the road.

"Yea, I'm sure, auntie."

Eternity was used to having her own set of wheels ever since she had gotten her license. There was no way she was going without her own. She loved the luxury of getting up and going anywhere that she had wanted to because she had her own shit to ride in. When she went out, the option of leaving was up to her, and she liked it that way.

She already felt like she was taking seventeen steps back in life, there was no way she would take another by not having her own car.

"You also need to find a doctor out here. I see you still limping round on that foot. You need to take care of you."

Eternity shook her head up and down as she agreed. She knew that her healing process was supposed to be better than what she was experiencing. She was sure that she had injured her foot more with her late-night escapades to visit her son at the graveyard but, she didn't care.

Nora pulled into the dealership and parked. The two ladies exited the car, and as soon as they did, salesmen came up to them—all with different pitches that all ended the same way. Buy a car from us. Eternity's eyes met with a champagne-colored Tesla, and her heart melted. She had the money to get one, but then she thought about this new leaf that she was turning over.

2015 had been the absolute worst year for her. She brought it in with Bleek and felt so much love, and then it ended tragically. She was taking 2016 to start all the way over, she needed a clean fucking slate. Matter fact, she needed a new slate. It was close to impossible cleaning the old slate called year 2015. It didn't matter how much Awesome degreaser or Ajax she used. The grime from that year was stuck.

A new slate needed to be purchased, and that's what 2016 would be for her. She sighed as she tore her eyes away from the Tesla.

"Take me to where the Nissans are. I want an Altima. Let me tell you exactly what I want."

Eternity went on to say the year that she wanted, the color, and even the added extras. When she had purchased her very first car, she learned that when walking into a dealership that you had to have your mind made up. You had to have your shit together because if you didn't, them vultures in the lot would talk your head off and then empty your pockets.

Eternity followed the salesman to the Nissan section. Once they got to the section Eternity, saw the exact car that she had wanted and in her favorite color, midnight blue. In a matter of two hours, she was out of the dealership. Finally, she felt some sense of freedom. Finally, she felt like things were getting back on track. Still, she felt the void in her chest every time she thought of her son, but starting over was making things a little bit easier.

She needed to get back to her. Fuck that she deserved to get back to her after the loss that she had taken, she needed this more than anything.

"I see you, baby girl, I see you pushing this nice new car, okay. Now let's go get that job." Auntie Nora said to Eternity as she switched lanes on the expressway.

"All right, auntie, show me how to get there. Direct me," she said to her when she stopped at the next light.

Nora looked around the car and admired the new technology that the inside held. They had just come back from parking her car back at the house, and now they were onto their next adventure. Looking at the digital dashboard, she half the mind to get her a nice little upgraded car from the 2001 Intrepid that she was riding around in.

"Okay, I'ma tell you where to go. Oooo, I really like this new car you got the blueteeth in here. I wanna play my music."

"The what auntie Nora?" Eternity chuckled out as she asked. She was amused by her aunt.

"The music thing. I said it wrong, didn't I?" Nora could tell that by the expression on Eternity's face that she had messed up on something.

"It's *Bluetooth,* Auntie Nora. Press the Bluetooth button on your phone, and it should automatically connect." Eternity knew that Nora was connected to the Bluetooth once she heard the soothing sounds of Tina Turner...

You must understand though the touch of your hand
Makes my pulse react
That it's only the thrill of boy meeting girl
Opposites attract
It's physical
Only logical
You must try to ignore that it means more than that ooo

"What's love got to do with it, got to do with it."
Nora sang.
Eternity couldn't help but join in.

"What's love but a second-hand emotion."

The two women sang the song as if they had written it.

They ended their travels in the parking lot of a Kroger's. Eternity found a park out front, and then she and her aunt exited the car.

"This is where you work, auntie?" Eternity asked Nora as they slowly started to walk towards the supermarket.

"Sure do. I work the machines in the back overnight. When we walk in there, I'm going to let you know who you need to speak to while I go and get my check but remember boo you need this. It's obvious that you don't need it for the money, but please do this for your own peace of mind. Trust me, you know I know what you're going through right now and baby, you can either let that pain make or break you, don't let it be the ladder."

Eternity sighed and then made her depart from her aunt. She walked to one of the offices and then asked for a supervisor that was on shift. She was directed to sit in one of the chairs in the hallway and wait on one of the personnel from HR. Her palms were sweating, and she didn't understand why, especially considering that this was something that she didn't even want in the first place.

"Ms. Washington?" a man stepped out of one of the offices and called out.

"Yes, that's me."

Eternity stood from the seat and then ran her hand down her dark denim jeans. She knew that she probably should have had on business attire, but she didn't pack any, and then the day had gone by so fast that she wasn't able to stop for any clothes.

"Come on in."

The man held the door open for her. After making sure that she had walked into the room, he closed the door behind her.

*CC*hapter 11

Two months later …

Man-Man winced in pain as he slowly strolled through his establishment. The End Zone was set to open in just three weeks, but he wasn't looking forward to the festivities. His recovery was a slow one, and his main concern was the mental and physical state of Tori. He slid into the booth and then found comfort on the black padded seat. He pulled his phone out of his pocket to check the time. He hated anyone being late, and there wasn't a doubt in his mind that Nova knew that.

Since he had left the hospital, he knew that he had to sit down with her. For as long as he knew her, the temperament of her vibe was always stoic. She seemed bothered, and he could just tell that her dangerous lifestyle had everything to do with it.

Because his new sports bar was still technically a construction site, he knew that meeting her there would be the perfect location. The workers were busy, and there were no outsiders to catch a glimpse of her. All of this, he thought of because he wouldn't be himself if he didn't constantly worry about the well-being of others. Especially those he had love for.

She had lasted this long in the game by being a ghost, and he wouldn't risk what she had worked so hard to build. Even though he disagreed with the shit.

"You're looking better these days, Marcelo." Man-Man smiled slightly at the sarcasm in her voice. He had caught a whiff of her Dior perfume before she had even uttered a word. Although he wasn't facing the door, he knew when she had entered the space.

The click of her heels echoed in his ears with each step. He heard it over the electrical saw going and over the chatter of the construction workers. Her dainty frame slid into the booth. She placed her Birkin bag onto the table and then put her elbows onto the same surface after it. She rested her chin onto the back of her hands and then tilted her head slightly. Her natural coils fell into the front of her face.

Quickly she swiped away the honey blonde streaked tresses.

"Come on… what mess are you in?"

Crinkles formed in the bridge of Nova's nose before she responded.

"Can I look at you and appreciate the progress of your recovery before we get into that bullshit?"

"I'm breathing… Now, what have you gotten yourself into." Man-Man took a deep breath before he continued, "And how can I help?"

He knew that whatever mess she had gotten herself into had to be huge. She had almost every means to make any and every situation disappear, so if she was stuck between a rock and a hard place, the situation was bad. When the silence lingered between them for too long, Man-Man took a sip of his water so that he could take his pain killers. The scarred tissue in his throat still bothered him from time to time, but he was stubborn, so he refused a second surgery.

"I killed the postmaster general."

Water and the oxycodone he had just attempted to take flew out of his mouth and landed onto the table. He started to cough profusely. Quickly Nova stood from her seat and then rounded the table to pat him onto his back. When he finally caught his breath, he cleared his throat.

"What the fuck you mean you killed a man," he whispered.

He didn't care that it was the postmaster general, he couldn't picture her killing any man.

"I had to."

Pain eluded across her glossy pupils as she whispered.

Construction workers started to walk past, so Man-Man stood and then motioned for Nova to follow behind him. They needed privacy. When they reached his office, he closed the door behind him and then leaned up against his French imported oak desk that was still tightly secured in bubble wrap. Even his office wasn't ready for the upcoming grand opening. All of the drama in his life lately had halted his progress. Him getting shot, him worrying about Tori since Eternity had left and now Nova. Every situation that stood in-between him and the grand opening of his next establishment to him was all worth it. He would pause his own success to make sure that those around him were stable.

"Why didn't you call me sooner. I saw his suicide on the news months ago, Nova Lee... what the fuck."

She started pacing the wooden planks as she rubbed the palms of her hands together. They began to feel clammy from her sweat.

Her sin was one that her sisters didn't even know of. The only other person besides her cleaner that was responsible for staging deaths that knew about this deed was now Man-Man.

"I didn't see sense in telling you."

Man-Man tilted his head sideways. Before love and marriage, he and Nova shared a friendship first. Even after the signed divorce papers still, because of business, they held a close-knit relationship.

He didn't share with Tori how close their relationship still was out of fear. To him, most women wouldn't and couldn't understand the bond that he still had with his ex-wife. After casually dating before Tori and hitting brick walls with other women on the topic, he stopped expecting women to understand. Nova was the kind of woman that even if you could control your sexual urges around her, you still needed that friendship from her. Her vibe was unmatched, and when she loved you, it was endless.

At their prime, their mental connection was one that Man-Man told himself that he would never want to lose. He may have lost his wife to the game that he escaped so effortlessly, but he would have never wanted to lose his friend.

"Why?" He questioned.

Nova huffed before she answered his question. Her short legs stopped walking, ending her travels directly in front of him.

"I didn't see sense in telling you because—"

"Na fuck that… why did you do it?"

Nova blinked and then put some space in-between her and him. Still so in love, she needed some kind of space while around him—a blocker to control herself.

"I don't know how, but he found out about my whole operation. He found out how I was moving Heavenz through the mail. He knew how my sisters were connected and how you and Vincent were as well. I set a meeting with him, and I swear I had all intentions to handle the situation peacefully, but when he couldn't get what he wanted from me…"

Nova stared off into the corner of the room. Her eyes misted as she thought back to the night where she had to do what she had to. She was protecting those around her, and at the moment, she was protecting herself.

Never in her life had she had to protect herself against a man, but that night she had to. With her bodyguard only a couple of feet away on the other side of the hotel suite door, she was about to be violated. If the game had taught her nothing else, she learned that she had to fend for herself. Growing up, she never had to. She always had her sisters, but with her deciding to stay in the game shifted things in her mind when it came to them.

They both voluntarily left. They wanted to, and being that Nova was addicted to the lifestyle, she wouldn't dare reach out to them when it concerned just that. She felt her chin being cupped, and then suddenly, her face was turned to the left—her brown orbs connected with his dual-colored ones.

"The fuck did that fat white ass man want from you? I know it wasn't money cause his ass had to be loaded, and if he wanted to be crooked, you should have cut a deal with him, Nova Lee, not kill him."

"He wanted me, he forced himself on me in that hotel room."

She closed her eyes, and when she did tears slid down her face. Man-Man wrapped his strong arms around her petite frame and then pulled her into his embrace. She cried into his chest. Finally, she was breaking that Teflon exterior she had built up over the years.

For months she held this pain in. She couldn't even count since the incident, how many times her sisters asked her what was wrong. To keep them out of the game, she kept her lips sealed. She knew that if she uttered anything of that night to her big sisters that they would come running headfirst back into what they didn't want any parts of. So, she carried this burden all on her own. Damn, it felt good to release, especially in the arms of someone that she trusted.

"I didn't even know what the fuck to do, so I shot him before he could do anything." She cried out.

"Shhh, shhh," he hushed her.

Man-Man placed his chin onto the top of her head and then sighed deeply. This is exactly why he had wanted her out of the game. It didn't have any rules, and it was ruthless, especially when it came to women. He knew that the average drug dealer or even king pin knew better than to try Nova that way. But, that cooperate suit-wearing face of the federal government mail system didn't know or didn't care to treat Nova with the respect that the rest of the corrupt black-market drug trade world would.

"Your cleaner did a good job at staging the suicide. Why are the cops looking for you?"
He had to know. Officers were staking out his places of business and his home because of this.

"Emanuel did very well, but somehow they know that I was the last to meet with him. I don't know who that bastard told that we had a meeting set, but they know." Man-Man sighed and then shook his head from left to right. The feeling of the strands of her hair tickled the skin under his chin.

"How can I help you?"

Nova broke their embrace because what she was about to ask went against everything that Man-Man stood for, and she knew it. He tried his best to keep his distance when it came to himself and law enforcement, but she needed him to be in their space. She needed an alibi, and her ex-husband would be the best one.

"I'm tired of running Marcelo I know that they have been looking for me for the past three months. I need an alibi, and I need it to be you. I want to come to the states and not have to look over my damn shoulder. I already told my lawyer my plans of putting this to rest, and he is certain that everything can get handled without even seeing the inside of a courtroom."

Man-Man massaged the tension out of his neck.

"You can't use one of your sisters as an alibi?"

He didn't want to involve himself in shit, but he knew that he would only if she *needed* him to.

"They don't even know that I murdered the man. Even if they did because they are my sisters, they are the worst alibi to use. The cops are expecting them to protect me. As my ex-husband, they aren't expecting you to do the same."

"Okay…"

"Okay?" She questioned.

She thought that she would have to pitch her plan some more before she received his approval.

"Yea, whenever you want to do this, just call me, and I got it. I can say you were with me inside. I ordered Chinese food that night for my girl and me, I can say that it was for you and me. If worst comes to worst, I'm cool with the delivery boy. I can say that you opened the door to get the food, and if they need to ask him have he seen you, I can break him off a little change to say he did."

The corners of Nova's mouth turned upward. She loved the shit out of the man in front of her.

"I can pay the delivery boy. You're already helping me. I don't need you to spend money. That can go towards your little one that's on the way."

Man-Man was about to ask how she knew that he was expecting to be a dad soon, but quickly he remembered that Tori and ex-wife had crossed paths while he was in the hospital.

"Don't do that, I said what I said."

Man-Man finally leaned off of his desk and then stood tall.

He towered over Nova's frame. Their conversation had come to an end; she was dreading it. As she looked up at him, only two words came to her mind.

"Thank you," she whispered.

"We always gone be family Nova, you good."

He kissed the top of her head and then started to head towards the door.

"I gotta get back home…"

Home, she missed when she was home for him. She closed her eyes for a moment and then breathed deeply before fluttering those lids open again.

Man-Man held the door to his office open and waited for her to walk out. Once she did, he had walked out behind her. Together they exited his place of business. A black-tinted Escalade waited for her outside. He walked her to her car and then waited for her to get inside. When she did, he walked over to his car and then got in. He watched as her car peeled off out of the parking lot. The alarm on his phone went off, letting him know that it was time for him to take his antibiotics. He turned his thirty-minute drive home into fifteen.

*C*hapter 12

Tori heard keys jingling in the door, and a smile appeared across her face. She turned her body to the side so that she could get a better view of the front door from in the living room where she sat.

"How are you feeling, love?"

Man-Man sat on the couch next to her, and naturally, she placed her feet into his lap.

Those foot rubs that he gave were everything to her. The pad of his thumb massaged the arch in her foot in a circular motion.

"Mmm, that feels good."

Tori threw her head back as she groaned.

"How are you feeling, love?" He asked again.

Lately, she had been up and down. An unpredictable mess since her sister has left town. Luckily a few weeks ago, Tori's aunt had given her a call to let her know that Eternity was well, breathing, and working. At least now, Tori could breathe a little, knowing that her sister was in a better headspace.

Still, she yearned for her sister's love. She wanted her sister's guidance, especially when it came to this pregnancy thing. There she was seven months solid, and she felt lost. She needed that motherly advice and her sister, and only her sister could give her that.

"I've been better. Especially now knowing that she's okay. I just kind of wish that she was here for this, you know." Tori said as she rubbed her stomach.

Together they were alone in this thing. Adding to their family, it was only them. She thought that in her life, when she would be bringing life into this world that she would have her sister and at least her child's father's family, but like her, Man-Man didn't have much family. Tori knew that once she delivered their beautiful baby girl that she would feel so much better. Their baby girl would fill all of her voids. All she needed was that extra being to love on.

"How is the bar coming along?"

"It's coming out good."

Man-Man's response was short. He toyed with the thought of telling Tori everything that Nova had told him, but he didn't. He couldn't. He was the kind of man that held everyone's secrets. He was the secret keeper, and at times it put him at a disadvantage. He hoped that him omitting his participation in helping Nova didn't come back to bite him in the ass.

"I think I want to go to Atlanta to see her."

Tori was tired of getting updates from her aunt every other day. She needed to see her sister to physically see how she was doing.

"When are we going?" He asked.

"We?"

Man-Man raised his eyebrow and then stopped massaging Tori's foot.

"Yea, we. You too far in this pregnancy to be flying, let alone by yourself." He confirmed.

Tori exhaled in a sigh. She had been thinking about visiting her sister for days. Being that Man-Man had been running around ever since he was discharged from the hospital, she hadn't factored him in.

"You seem to be so busy with this new bar that I didn't want to take you from business."

"Our family affairs is my business."

He shut her the fuck up. To go on a journey while pregnant with his child wasn't one that he was willing to allow her to take alone. Hell, even if she wasn't pregnant still, he would tag along because, to him, mental health was important.

He knew how his girl wore her heart on her sleeve, and with the extra hormones pumping through her, he knew that the uninvited visit could go one of two ways. Either good or very bad and deep down inside, he prayed that it wouldn't be the latter. When he noticed that the corners of her mouth turned upward, he continued to massage her foot.

"Go ahead and set a flight up for tomorrow if you can."

He slightly lifted his lower body from the couch and then pulled his wallet out of his back pocket. He handed it to her.

"Take the black card out and book the tickets."

Tori did what she was told, all with a smile on her face. Shit like that is what she loved. Her man was the definition of a boss. Besides his swagger and mentality, the invite-only charge card in his wallet was an indication of that. She loved herself a black man that had his shit together.

Man-Man's phone started to ring. When he pulled it from his pocket, the name on the face made his eyebrows dip, which caught the attention of Tori. Quickly the smile she was wearing while scrolling the Expedia website had faded. *Nova. What is she doing calling?* The same exact thought crossed both of their minds. Man-Man tapped Tori's legs twice.

"Watch out bae, I need to take this."
Tori moved her feet from his lap but didn't utter a word.

There had to be a valid reason as to why his ex-wife was calling him. *Maybe she's just checking on him after the shooting,* she thought. *Na, fuck that. Why would he need to leave the room for that? She is the connect, maybe it's business. Na, fuck that he been out of the game, there should be no reason for a private conversation.*

Tori's thoughts ran full speed through her mind. She sniffled. Those damn tears were always on the horizon with her. That was the only thing she hated thus far about this thing called pregnancy. She used the back of her hand to wipe away her tears. After taking a deep breath, she found a flight that was suitable for her. She was happy when she saw that it was only one seat left. Quickly she purchased the ticket and then placed Man-Man's card onto the coffee table.

As she was walking up the stairs to pack, he was coming down.

"Your card is on the coffee table," she said dryly.

"Okay, I gotta make a run really quick. I'll be back later with some food, okay?"

He was rushing. His feet were moving quickly down the stairs, and his words were just as quick as his steps. Standing at the top of the stairs, Tori looked down at him.

"Mmm-hmm."

She was going to tell him about her flight for the next day and how only she was going, but she decided not to. She made it up in her mind that she would have that talk with him when he returned home.

"Take your antibiotics before you *rush* out."

She said just before she turned and headed towards their bedroom. She was satisfied when she heard the pills in the bottle knocking together from Man-Man taking one. Seconds later, she listened to their front door close. She stood in the window of their bedroom and watched as he rushed out to his car. He quickly backed out of the driveway and then sped down the block.

The last tear had fallen, and Tori used one finger to wipe it away. She made it up in her mind that when he returned that they would speak on this Nova situation. They had never lacked communication skills, and she wasn't about to start holding back shit now. She finally pulled herself from the window and then headed towards her closet. Even after their talk, still, she figured that she would need some time away from him. She needed to be around her sister.

Man-Man tapped the steering wheel as he made his way to the jailhouse. He knew Nova so well. Her tone of voice on the phone was steady, but he could sense the fear in it. Finally, the inevitable had happened. She had gotten pinched. How could a woman that moved like a ghost finally get caught up? He knew that it was because of him. She was cold-hearted, but when it came to him, she turned into putty. It was the biggest flaw in her that he had noticed years ago, but he never addressed it. If anything, that one flaw let him know that she was still human.

Her showing her emotions when it came to him let him know that deep down inside, a beating heart still remained within her frame.

"Fuck!" He roared as he slapped the top of his steering wheel.

Pretty girls like Nova didn't belong in jail. Knowing that once you were on the federal scope that it was hard as hell to get off, he knew that he would have to call her sisters.

He see-sawed in his mind on who he should call to relay the news. There was no way that Nova would have given them a call, he knew that her pride wouldn't even bring her to reach out to them for help, especially since it was her decision, and hers only to remain in the game.

He took his chances with Nova's older sister Jayde. He figured that she would be the easier one to talk too. While at a traffic light, he hovered over her name with his thumb. He hated to be chastised, and he was sure that it was coming. After sighing, he pressed the name and then waited for the ringing sounds to fill the speakers to his car.

"Hello, Marcelo." She answered on the fourth ring. He just knew that she was probably standing over her phone, watching it ring. She had always been the type to practice social distancing.

"Hey, Jayde. Nova's in trouble."

He heard rustling in his ear before he listened to the urgency in her tone.

"What do you mean? Matter fact hold on. Let me conference Yoli in."

Before Man-Man could object, Jayde had put him on hold. This is what he didn't want. He didn't want to speak to the middle sister at all. She had never taken a liking to him, and although she never uttered anything disrespectful his way out of love and respect for her younger sister, her tone couldn't be cloaked in anything that wasn't authentic because that was just how she rolled.

"Yoli?"

"Yea I'm here."

"Marcelo."

"Yeah..."

"Okay, now go. How is Nova in trouble?"

Man-Man held the steering wheel with one hand while gently massaging his temple with the other.

"She got arrested."

"What?" Yoli screeched.

"Where? In Chattanooga?" Jayde's tone was cool. She held that big sister demeanor—that calm shit. Even in times of crisis, she had to remain level-headed because she knew that if she didn't, then Yoli would freak out.

"Yea, she's out here I'm on my way to the county jail now. She called me from her phone there."

"What is she even doing in fucking Tennessee?" Yoli asked.

Then is when Man-Man knew that Nova was flying solo. She usually moved in threes. There wasn't much that her sisters didn't know about her movements, but something told him that lately, she had been distancing herself from them. The corrupt game had forced her to be this way. Just when Man-Man was about to answer the question that Yoli had asked, Jayde had spoken.

"We're past that sis. We just need to get there. Marcelo, we will be there by tomorrow. Keep us updated if anything changes."

"See, this is the shit that I was talking about when I said her ass should have left with us. But nooo she just couldn't leave shit alone—"

"Marcelo, you can hang up." Jayde interrupted Yoli to get him off the phone.

Yoli's rant was the last thing that Jayde wanted to hear, so she knew that Man-Man didn't want to partake in it either. Without saying a word, he ended the line just as he was pulling up to the county jail.

Chapter 13

After spending the later of the afternoon packing, straightening up the house, and then taking a couple of naps, Tori was still left in the house by herself. She gathered her late-night snacks and placed them onto the island in the kitchen. This was her routine. Ice cream cones and sour patch kids were her things when 3 a.m rolled around.

Man-Man was usually the one to prep her after-hours snack, but he had yet to come home. All she could think about was the last call to his cellphone that he received before he left. A call from Nova. What would keep him out this late, and why with no response? His phone had been going to voicemail, and inwardly it made her cringe. At this time of night, only two things in Chattanooga was open: gas stations and legs.

In her arms, she tried to balance her tray of snacks and her cellphone. While walking up the carpeted steps, her flip flop bent on one stair. Leaving her chubby toes on one stair while the slipper on the one beneath. This threw her balance off, causing her to stumble back down the stairs. The full tray of snacks hit the bottom level of the home before her body did. The impact of her body hitting the floor of the foyer rattled her core. Her warm body was met with the cold feel of the tiles.

Instantly she felt a pain in her stomach that she had never felt before. She didn't care about the ice cream that she had landed on, her number one concern was her baby. As she laid on the floor, she let one of her hands trail down to her stomach, and it felt hard as a rock. A cry escaped her frame when she started to feel contractions.

"Fuckkkkk. No, no, no, no!" She groaned.

She breathed deeply with every contraction that she felt. Luckily her cell phone had landed next to her body. She reached for it and noticed that her screen was now cracked. She quickly tried to call Man-Man, but when the phone went to voicemail like expected, she knew that her next call had to be to 911. She needed an ambulance because the pain she felt was unbearable, and for some strange reason, her body was fighting against her about getting off of the floor.

"Mam, are you able to open the door for the ambulance when they arrive?" The man on the phone asked.

She tried once more to lift her body up from the floor, but when she was unsuccessful, she cried out in response.

"No, I can't. I'm stuck on the floor."

She knew that emergency services would have to break down her door.

"Okay, mam, try to remain calm and still. Help will be there soon, okay?"

"Okay."

As the phone hung up in Tori's ear, she tried to control her breathing, but with each contraction, she was losing control.

"Siri, call Eternity…" she called out.

"Calling Eternity…"

The phone rung twice and then went to voicemail. She ended the line and then tried to call the next best person that could possibly keep her calm in this situation.

"Siri, call Bleek…"

"Calling Bleek…"

Instead of being met with ringing, she was met with an automated message.

"We're sorry the number you have reached has been temporarily disconnected…. Goodbye."

When the line ended, Tori silently cried to herself. She started to count in her head, and when she got to number three hundred, she felt wetness in between her legs. Tori bit her bottom lip as pain radiated through her body. When she got to number three hundred and twenty, she heard the sound of her front door being knocked open. Two paramedics came into her peripheral vision.

"Mam, how long ago did your water break?"

"My water broke?" She started to panic.

"Okay, mam, try, and stay relaxed. How far are you?"

"28 weeks."

"Okay, stay calm. We are gonna get you help, okay?" The two paramedics lifted Tori onto the stretcher and then carried her out.

The sun was high in the sky when Man-Man went to put the key into the front door to his home. He paused when he saw that the lock was broken. He went for his back waistband, but when he came up empty, he remembered that he locked his gun inside of the glove compartment of his car before entering the jailhouse the night before. He looked back at his car and had thoughts on retrieving it, but then he thought of Tori being inside when whoever had broken in.

With no protection of his own, he rushed into his home.

"Tori," he yelled.

Not caring what waited for him inside. Right at the stairs, he saw a pool of liquid mixed with blood and snacks on the floor of the foyer.

"Tori," this time, he said with more base in his voice. He skipped over the puddle on the floor and then skipped up the stairs. After checking all of the rooms upstairs and coming up empty, he rushed downstairs to the basement.

He had cameras on the outside of his residence, and he was sure that they would tell him what happened the night before. Man-Man rewound the footage and then plugged his dead phone into a nearby charger. When he came back to the television, he saw Tori standing outside, dragging the garbage bins to the curb. He grew annoyed because he knew that she knew that garbage was his responsibility.

He blew out a sharp breath as he watched Tori wobble her way back into the house. He fast-forwarded the footage until he saw an ambulance truck pull onto his property. His phone that had just turned back on started to erupt into numerous alerts. Man-Man rushed over to his phone and saw all of the voicemails from Tori's phone. He looked at the television and saw two ambulance workers hauling Tori out of the front door as he played the last voice message he had gotten from her.

"Marcelo fucking Bridges, if your daughter beats you here, there will be a problem. She's coming now. Argggggghhhh. Where are you?"

Man-Man ran out of the house and then hopped in his car. As he raced to the hospital, he thought of the night before. He should have been home, but he wasn't. When trying to be a good friend, a good ex-husband, it turned around to bite him in the ass. He would never forgive himself if he missed the birth of his daughter. *It's too damn soon,* he thought to himself as he weaved in and out of morning traffic. His daughter wasn't supposed to be on the way yet, Tori wasn't at full term.

"Fuck!" he roared as he thought of the night before.

"Thank you for picking me up from the jailhouse."

Nova kicked out of her sneakers, took off her socks, and then wiggled her toes across the plush carpet as she made her way to the bathroom. She ran the shower water and then pulled her hair out of the bun that she was just wearing.

"It was no problem. I told you they would probably want to just question you."

Man-Man stood with his arms hugged around his frame. He stood in an uncomfortable stance.

Nova stood in the doorway of the bathroom and sensed his uncomfortableness.

"I just wish you wouldn't have called my sisters before getting all of the information about my arrest. Now tomorrow I have to have this long drawn out conversation with them."

"You better tell them what you did too."

Nova remained quiet. She dreaded coming clean to her sisters, but she knew that she had to.

"I know," she admitted.

She sighed before she unbuttoned her jeans.

"I'm about to shower really fast. Something about the county jail just makes me feel gross. You're welcome to sit and get comfortable."

"Nah, I think Ima head out…"

"Marcelo, please. I really thought that I was about to get bagged for murder can you at least stay until I fall asleep."

Man-Man checked the time on his Audemars and then sighed. It was eleven at night, but he took a seat in a nearby chair anyway.

"Hurry up and shower and then come bring ya ass to bed. I gotta get home."

Nova smiled, entered the bathroom, and then closed the door behind her. Man-Man took out his phone and then started to check the many emails that he had when it came to his new sport's bar. He wished that Tori wasn't experiencing a high-risk pregnancy because then she would have been able to hire all of the staff that he needed.

That was her job, she ran his first sport's bar effectively. He wished that she was in the proper state to run this one. He checked over resumes and saw candidates that he would have never hired. Just when he caught an attitude with the list of people that had applied to the vacant positions, Nova came out of the bathroom.

The white bathrobe swallowed her frame. Her hair that was just silky straight was now puffy due to the humidity from her shower.

"Thought you would have snuck out when I was in the shower." She said jokingly.

"Now, why would I do that when you asked me to stay?"

"Well, shit, I don't know."

Nova climbed into the bed with her statement. After tucking her body under the covers, Man-Man yawned, which caused Nova to yawn.

She reached onto the nightstand, grabbed the remote, and then turned on the television. Basketball highlights is what she remembered as a past time favorite of theirs. Nova tossed the remote on the other side of the bed where Man-Man could reach from the chair he sat in, and then she got comfortable in the bed.

Man-Man slowly opened his eyes. When he pulled his cellphone out of his pocket, he saw that it was dead. He stood from the chair and then stretched. When he looked over at a sleeping Nova, her petite mouth was wide open as she lightly snored. He didn't remember her being a snorer. When he looked over at the nightstand and saw that the time on the nightstand said 6:23 a.m., he hurried out of the room and then rushed to his car. The blackout curtains in the room hid the sunrays that he was met with when he exited the hotel...

As Man-Man found a park in labor and delivery, he banged on the steering wheel once more before getting out of the vehicle. He stepped out of the elevator on the labor and delivery floor. When he rushed into the room that the receiptionist had given him, he saw that Tori was sleep.

"They were finally able to get her down." A nurse said as she looked at the monitors that were hooked to Tori.

"Get her down?" he asked as he took the seat beside Tori's bed.

"Yup, she had to be sedated. She pushed out a stillborn and then—"

"She did what!?"
Because of the heavy sedatives that Tori was under the roar of Man-Man did not wake her.

"Where is my daughter?" he asked quickly, regaining his composure.

"I am so sorry sir. I'll go and get the doctor for you."

Man-Man stood from his seat with pleading eyes.

"Please, just tell me where my baby girl is?"
The mist that covered his dual covered eyes tugged at the nurse.

"She had to deliver a stillborn baby. Your daughter is in the morgue here at the hospital. I will still go and get the doctor for you."

Man-Man held onto the arm of the chair for support. His eyes drifted over to a sleeping Tori in the bed, and that's when he let the tears fall from his eyes. *She is never going to forgive me for not being here for this.* He thought as he used the back of his closed fist to wipe away his emotions.

Chapter 14

The season had flipped over twice, and Bleek had found some sense of peace. The month of October was busy, with customers still redeeming their Labor Day promotions. Long days filled with engine oil and signing documents had become the daily routine for Bleek. It was the only thing that seemed to take the heavyweight off his chest. That grief was so suffocating, and at any moment, if he thought about it for too long, then he fell into a state of depression. If he wasn't at one of his shops, then his time was wrapped up in Paris.

She was the perfect distraction. She was a healer, and slowly, she was healing him. He was finally letting her in, and the more he let her into his world, the more he questioned why he hadn't done so sooner. The highlights of his day lately were the parts where he would come home to her or go home, and then she would come home to him. His life was finally experiencing some normalcy, and he was embracing it.

As he stepped off the elevator, he grabbed his house keys out of his jacket pocket. The closer he got to his door, he saw that it was slightly open. He stopped in his tracks and then pulled his phone from the other pocket. Bleek was never the paranoid type, but with him digging deeper into who had robbed him the Christmas before last, he knew that there was only a matter of time before someone came his way. His heart was beating out of his chest as the phone rang in his ear.

Suddenly, he remembered that downstairs the doorman wasn't at his post. There were times when the man would take a break and abandoned the desk, but Bleek had a sickening feeling in his gut about the man's absence. When the call went to voicemail, he put his house keys back into the pocket of his jacket since it wasn't needed. He placed the call again, and it was answered on the second ring.

"Hello?" Paris answered in a hushed tone.

"Where are you?" The urgency in Bleek's voice told her that something was wrong.

"I'm sitting in on a court case, that's why I didn't answer the first time. Is everything okay?"

"Yea... when you done come to the address that I'm going to text you. Do not come back to my condo, okay..."

Although she wanted to poke at the whys, she decided on doing the opposite.

"Okay."

"Aight I gotta go…"

Bleek ended the line and then pulled his gun from his waistband. Slowly he crept towards his ajar front door. With his unoccupied hand, he pushed the door open. Still, his weapon was pointed forward. He walked into his living quarters and saw that it was trashed. His living room television was off the wall and smashed onto the floor. Even his couch was turned over. He walked as lightly as he could. Slowly he stepped over broken glass. He wanted to clear his entire apartment before he let his guard down and put his gun away.

Once he reached his master bedroom and saw that the room was trashed too, he moved onto his bathroom. The mirror to the vanity was cracked, and in red lipstick on the mirror, *"Chiva Blanca"* was written. He studied how the end of the "a" in the word Blanca curved and then formed a small heart. He never thought that the person he had been chasing these past few months was a woman, but the masterpiece of destruction in front of him confirmed it.

He sighed and then tucked his gun back into his waistband. He was being watched, and he knew it. He was so strictly observed that his enemy knew where he rested his head, and that didn't sit well with him. A change was going to have to come, and no longer staying in his condo was one of them. It was time that he stripped that fairytale picture of him sharing his home with his possible wife. Right now, Paris was in the picture, and he had no intention of erasing her out the frame. That and he wouldn't allow himself to possibly put her in harm's way. Under his roof, he knew that he had a better advantage of protecting her. If he was going to stay at his house in Coral Gables, so was she.

~~~~~~

Tori tossed and turned inside of the bed. Next to her was a vacant spot. The digital clock that stood on the nightstand to her left was the only form of lighting that illuminated the darkroom. 3:45 a.m., and he was still not home. Tori flipped the covers off of her frame and then sat up in the bed. Since her miscarriage, she had seen the decline in their relationship, but this was her last straw.

She was sick and tired of Man-Man's long nights. She felt like purposely since their loss that he had tried his hardest to distance himself from her. She knew that it probably had everything to do with him not wanting to talk about his absence on that night. She had missed her flight to Atlanta when she had her miscarriage, so she randomly re-scheduled her trip. Her plane was due to leave in just three hours, and before she had gone to bed the night before, she was hopeful that she would be able to see Man-Man to speak with him before she left.

She snatched her phone off of the charger and then placed a call to his phone. Instead of ringing, she was immediately met with the sound of his voicemail. She sucked her teeth and then put her phone back on the nightstand. There was no way that she could go back to sleep with this troubled mind. Since losing her daughter, she begged God for emotions, she wanted to feel anything. She blamed herself at times for the decline in their relationship. Had her bitter steel made emotions had caused a rift between them? She wondered. She wished that she could flip a switch before something broke that could not be fixed.

C. Wilson

She knew that the broken item would be her
relationship. Where Man-Man showed and felt all of the
emotions of the miscarriage, she was numb. Hadn't God
taken enough from her? Her nephew, her sister, left, and then
her very own child. Involuntarily she sniffled, tears fell from
her brown orbs, but the emotions attached to it was
nonexistent. She stood from the bed and then walked into her
bathroom. She decided to tend to her hair and then pack
whatever little items that she had missed while packing the
night before.

As the sun started to peak, Tori's tresses were neatly
laid bone straight. The ends of her dark maroon hair ended at
her shoulders. She was showered dressed and wheeling her
luggage down the stairs when the front door opened. Her
eyes met with his, and the guilt in his eyes told her more than
what she cared to ask. Man-Man had made it a habit to now
stay out. The curiosity in Tori wanted to ask him what was so
special about Nova that required his attention all night, but
she knew that the answer would go unanswered. When it
came to Nova, Man-Man never had the answers. He could
have been sleeping on the couch in his office at his new
sport's bar, and he was, but still, she would believe that he
was out with *her*.

177

She sighed when she reached the bottom step. She pulled the handle to her suitcase upward so that she could drag it to the front door.

"Where are you going?" He asked.

Over the months, she had threatened to go stay in a hotel, but she never did.

"To Atlanta," she said flatly.

"You're going without me?" he asked.

He, too, was spent with the makings of their relationship. What used to be so natural was now becoming forced.

"It's not like you had intentions of going anywhere. Your time was spent elsewhere last night."

The tone in Tori's voice was steady. Man-Man was looking for any kind of emotion in her words.

A piece of him wanted to pull the emotions from her. He had no intention of spending the night with Nova the day of Tori's miscarriage, and although nothing happened between them, he knew that Tori would never believe that. Lately, these nights were spent in self solitude either at one of his businesses or parked up somewhere in his car.

Knowing that she would never believe his whereabouts if he told the truth, he didn't speak on them at all. He kind of hoped that she would get angry, yell, want to fight him anything. But no, she stood in front of him, emotionless and unfazed. That's how he knew, he knew that the love between the two had faded.

"Can we talk about that?"

"About where you were last night?" – she chuckled – "Ain't shit to talk about."

She was so short with her response that it cut Man-Man slightly. Was she really done with him? Could he really be done with her? In such a short amount of time, their relationship had more stress than a little bit. He thought that maybe their love wasn't strong enough to bear the weight of all of the bullshit. Man-Man watched as Tori walked around him and then opened the front door that he had just closed.

"When are you coming back?"

With her hand still on the handle of the door, she stood. His question had paused her. With her back turned to him, she chewed on her bottom lip. *Am I really done?* She wondered to herself. When she turned around to face him, she saw the sorrow in his dual-colored pupils. A man that was once so vocal with her hadn't been saying much lately. He tilted his head to the side as he observed her, and she took note of that.

He was trying to read her. He always tilted that round head to the side when he was trying to do that. He couldn't though she was unreadable. This new Tori was like brail. You had to feel her, but he had stopped doing that months ago. Their connection had severed with the death of their daughter.

"I don't know *if* I'm coming back."
The sides of Man-Man's jaw clenched, and for a moment, it was amusing to Tori. She wondered if that was anger that she was detecting. The nerve of him. How could he have an attitude when he spent numerous nights out one for a fact she knew was with his ex-wife.

Instantly she looked at him with disgust. In her mind, even if she had checked out on her emotions, stepping out on their relationship should never be an option.

"If?" Man-Man questioned, "if you leave out of that door without a return date, then consider your return unwelcomed."

Tori raised one eyebrow. Was he testing her, or was he looking for a challenge? The slightest chuckle escaped her lips, which caused Man-Man to cringe. She walked in his direction, and for a moment, his heart fell into his stomach. *She does still care,* he thought. She opened the closet door that was to the left of him and took out one of her jackets.

After putting it on, she grabbed the handle to her suitcase and then walked out of the front door. She didn't even bother to close the entrance to the house behind her because she wanted him to see her walk away.

"Tori..."

He called out to her, but she never stopped her movements towards her G-Wagon. She tossed the suitcase into the back seat and then got in the driver's seat. His car was blocking her in, but she refused to say another word to him. She eased her vehicle up a little bit, cut her wheel all the way to left, and then backed out onto the grass.

"Tori, are you fucking serious? You're messing up the lawn!" Man-Man yelled as she left tire tracks on the grass.

She stuck her middle finger up, and on her way out, she sideswiped the side of his red Mercedes Benz.

"What the fuck!" she heard him yell just before she drove down the curb and then down the block.

Man-Man watched as her truck became smaller in size, the further she got down the road. He checked out the damage to his car and then sighed. *She'll be back,* he thought. That little moment during her exit showed emotion. Finally, he was getting a rise out of her. If he would have known that all it would take was a day of him being the nonchalant one, then he would have done it months ago.

He knew that when she returned that he would have to sit her down and explain everything between him and Nova. Nothing sexually happened between them that night, and he made it up in his mind as he was trying to wipe the black paint from Tori's car off of his driver's side door that he would do any and everything to convince Tori that nothing had happened. Spending the night with Nova was accidental. He regretted it. He hated that Tori had left, but he knew that she would be back, he looked at this time apart as something that was needed.

Man-Man shook his head and stopped wiping his car down when small drizzles started to fall from the sky. He didn't remember it raining in the forecast, but he found irony in it because it was fitting for the situation that he was now in. In an instant, the rain picked up, which caused him to lightly jog back into his house. Once he closed the door behind him and leaned up against it, he profoundly sighed. Thoughts of the night before came to him, and instantly he got angry for allowing Tori to leave. He had a crook in his neck from sleeping on the couch in his office, and he let her go for that.

Despite whatever terms they were on, he shouldn't have stayed the night out, and what he should have done before she walked out of that door was reassure her that the night before he wasn't with Nova. He rolled his neck around slowly in a circular motion. *Why the fuck did I just let her leave?* He thought to himself as he slowly walked up the stairs and to his bed.

Chapter 15

Tori stood in the airport, and in an instant, a wave of Deja vu hit her. Just two years ago she was waiting in an airport on her sister to come and get her so that she could start fresh. Two years ago, she was supposed to start a new and that she did, but shortly after all of the good, the bad and the tragic started to come. She breathed deeply as she grabbed her suitcase from the belt, pulled the handle upward, and then slowly drug the halfway empty luggage behind her.

She hadn't packed much because she didn't know if her spur of the moment adventure was a temporary thing. She still had so much weighing of options to do. She still had so much to reconsider. She was never the type to get it and keep it on her own as shallow as it may seem, she always had a go-getter in her corner. Her aunt took care of her after Eternity got arrested, then when Eternity came home, it was Bleek. After him, she went back to her sister for support and then straight into the arms of Man-Man.

As the warm Georgia sun graced her skin, she wondered if she could pull her life together like how her sister had done. She had heard from the lips of her aunt how well Eternity was doing. Now it was her turn to see it first-hand. The warm sun rays against her brown cheeks made her wonder if she would ever glow again.

She wondered if her lips would ever curve upward naturally and not by force how she had been doing the past couple of months. She wondered if she could weather the storm. Was she as strong as her sister? The sound of a car honking pulled her from her thoughts. She placed her hand above her arched eyebrows and squinted her eyes to see better.

She spotted Aunt Nora inside of a car leaning over towards the passenger side with her upper body, practically hanging out of the window.

"Come on, chile, I left my damn neckbones on." Tori smiled at her aunt's southern twang. She hurried to the car, tossed her suitcase into the trunk, and then sat passenger side in Nora's new ride. The new car smell invaded Tori's nostrils as she dramatically exhaled once the cool breeze from the air conditioner blew through her tresses.

"This car is nice and look at your damn hair. I can just tell that my sister got you together," Tori said with a smile.

Nora was now pushing a shiny black 2016 Kia Optima, a gift from Eternity, for helping her push through her emotional barriers. Where Nora would typically wear a tore up wig, she had long strands of black hair with natural silver streaks that ended at her back. Tori was finally able to see her aunt in her natural element, and she loved it.

"You like this shit? Huh?"
Nora shook her head from side to side lightly to show off the body that her hair held.

"She didn't want to come with you to get me from the airport?"

The sound of desperation could be heard in Tori's tone. Nora held a brief pause. She knew that allowing Tori to come without alerting Eternity could be messy, but this is the moment she was waiting for. She yearned for the two girls that she had a hand in raising that were now beautiful women to be in the same room.

In her eyes, Eternity had reached her part of healing over the months that had passed. Nora saw first-hand how much progress Eternity had made. She knew now that it was Tori's turn to heal, and she knew that Eternity was needed for that. Even as little girls, Eternity had always been the stronger of the two. She carried all of her problems and ordeals on her back.

Tori always needed her big sister to make it through.

"Auntie Nora... she didn't want to come with you?" Tori asked again this time with more hurt behind her words.

"She volunteered for some overtime in the day. She'll see you when she gets in."

Nora didn't have it in her heart to let Tori know that she had yet to tell Eternity about her surprise visit.

⁂

The rest of the drive to Nora's house was filled with an awkward silence. She knew that Eternity was due to walk through the door in just an hour. Although Nora was spicy, sassy, and harbored an, I don't give a fuck attitude. She was soft when it came to these two girls. So much, these girls reminded her of the relationship she once shared with her baby sister.

Eternity had all of the makings of her while Tori shared the same makings of Machina, their mother. This is why Nora was scared for Tori to recover from her pain. She saw with her own two eyes how her sister had healed from her love scars. She turned to the needle. She knew that her niece was way stronger than her younger sister, but still, she feared the worst, history repeating itself.

After getting Tori settled in the living room, Nora started to make plates. Eternity always had an appetite when she came home from work. Keys could be heard jingling in the door as Nora placed the final plate onto the dining room table. Eternity walked across the threshold, and instantly her muscles and bones started to ache.

All of these new-found pains that her job had given her she welcomed. The frigid temperatures of the coolers that she cleaned at work made her feel alive. She dropped her keys into the dish on the table that stood in the foyer before she even gave her attention to the figure sitting on the couch.

"Tori Tee?" she questioned.

Tori looked up from her phone and smiled when she saw her sister's tired eyes.

"Hey sis," she said with a smile.

Eternity took in her sister's new look, and Tori did the same. The natural curly short do that Eternity was now wearing fit her face so well. Nora was getting ready to explain why Tori was there, to begin with, but held her tongue when she saw the two women embrace.

"I'm glad you're doing better," Tori whispered as she hugged her big sister.

"Why didn't you bring my niece with you. How are you, new mommy?"

Eternity felt Tori's back heave up and down, so she knew that she was crying. Nora hadn't shared what Tori had recently been through because it was for Tori to tell. Tori cried harder on her sister's shoulder.

"Hey…. Hey shh shh shh. We can talk about it later." Eternity pulled away from their embrace and then looked Tori in the eyes.

"Ah hem," Nora cleared her throat.

Both women looked in her direction.

"I say we eat tonight, and then tomorrow y'all take a day to worry about all the other bullshit."

Both women smiled as they agreed. Together they walked to the dining table to join Nora. All of the ladies spent the night reminiscing on the past, the good memories only. Those dark memories that they had experienced were so tragic that no one even thought to bring it up. Having a night replaying their childhood made both Tori and Eternity wonder how their mother was doing. They hadn't heard from her in years, and she could have very much have been dead. Still, the thought of her not being made them think of her.

ℭhapter 16

Tori and Eternity sat in a booth at T.G.I.F. They had six empty martini glasses in front of them.

"See, it's about showing respect. You once told me that when it came to Vincent and me. Somewhere down the line, Man-Man had to lose respect for you to stay out all night and not come with an explanation."

Eternity wrapped her tongue around her straw and then took another sip after her statement.

"Here you go, ladies."

The waiter said as he placed a plate of traditional wings in front of them. The two ladies were spending the afternoon with wings and booze, the perfect comfort food to vent about their problems, by their problems, meaning Tori's issues.

"See, I don't see where the respect drifted off to. I got distant after we lost the baby, but that was after he stayed out all night with that bitch. How could he stay out all night into the next morning with his ex-wife while I was pushing our dead baby out?" How?"

Tori let her last word trail off.

Both she and Eternity took a sip from their drinks before she continued.

"I just don't know why and where things fucked up." Eternity looked deep into her younger sister's eyes. She was about to spit game to her like only a big sister could. Fuck that, she was about to spit game like only a woman that has come through the other side of the storm could.

"Look, Tori Tee, you got to learn to leave the table when love's no longer being served. It's one of two ways this situation could go. It's either you want to work things out with him, or you don't."

"But—"

"Aht… I don't want to hear *it's not that simple.* It's either you go back to try and work on or rebuild what y'all had, or you go back home for clarity and then break free. I know you, you're the kind that needs to know why. Before you level up, you need that closure."

Tori slightly screwed her face. To her, what Eternity had just said was an insult. Was she really that detectable? Everyone else around her was able to move on from a fucked up situation without needing closure. Why couldn't she?

"I mean, I guess," Tori stated without emotion.

She felt like she didn't need the closure to move on. Through long phone conversations with Nora before she came, Nora said something similar. *Your heart is too pure baby, you will always wonder why.* Nora's words played in her head, and to her, it was a crock of shit. Why should someone put themselves in a situation just for closure? Why slice open closing wounds just to get the source of the reason?

"So, what are you going to do?"

Eternity asked, breaking her from her thoughts.

"I don't even know yet. I'm only here until tomorrow, so I have a little bit more time to think about that."

"Only until tomorrow?"
The disappointment in Eternity's tone was evident.

"Yeah, I didn't want to take too much time. So, a nice little weekend getaway was it."

"Oh, okay. I kind of wished you would have stayed a little longer considering that your birthday is in three weeks.

Tori had forgotten about her own birthday. With everything going on, her birthday was the last thing on her mind. When Tori didn't offer a response, Eternity spoke again.

"Well, I guess that tonight will be the turn-up night for your day. I mean, I could come out to Chat too…"

Tori's eyes lit up at the mention of her sister coming back to the town.

"We can do that," Tori stated with a smile.

On the inside, she didn't even know if she wanted to go back. She picked up her cellphone from the table and then frowned when she didn't see a text or call from Man-Man. Although she had his number on the do not disturb list, she still wished that he would have shown initiative to reach out.

"Tori, did you hear me?"

"Uh, no, what did you say?"

"I said we are going to a lounge tonight, so I hope you brought cute clothes with you. I haven't been out in so long." Eternity admitted.

She went from the party girl to the homebound woman that focused on her bag. Still, with all of the money she had in her savings, she kept up with working. Along with helping Nora with some of the bills, she paid her phone bill and then saved everything else.

"I didn't bring shit to wear, really."

Tori wasn't expecting to go anywhere. She knew that her sister was healed physically by the way her body didn't limp as much, and from what Nora had told her, she knew that Eternity was healed emotionally as well. But could someone ever heal mentally from the amount of shit that Eternity had been through?

"So, I guess we're going shopping."
The smile that graced Eternity's face made the corners of Tori's mouth turn upward. The time they had spent together so far was refreshing for Tori's spirit. The shopping trip would just be the icing on the cake.

"I'm gonna need you to get your head out of that phone. We're supposed to be looking for you something to wear tonight," Eternity sighed.

Tori tossed her phone into the MCM purse that she carried on her forearm. Still, Man-Man had not reached out to her, and at this point, she didn't care if he did or didn't.

"It's hot as fuck down here, so I want at least my calves out tonight. I wanna show off my new tattoo anyway."

"New tattoo, let me see?"
Tori pulled up the leg to her sweatpant to show Eternity her masterpiece.

It was a teddy bear with baby blocks that spelled out the name Nalah.

"Is that what you named her?" Eternity asked.

"Yes."

"It's really beautiful, sis."

Eternity felt the gloomy cloud starting to come their way, so she quickly continued to speak.

"Okay, well, I got the perfect look for you."

Eternity fanned through the rack of maxi and bandage dresses. Being that they were going to a hookah lounge, the dress down attire would be appropriate.

"Look at these two," Eternity said as she took two hangers off of the rack and then help them up so that Tori could see what was hanging from them.

"Any one is fine, sis," Tori said with a smile.

Eternity remembered when they were younger, she loved having a little sister for this exact moment. To play dress up. After picking out tons of outfits for Tori and something for herself, she paid for everything. The buzz Eternity had from the restaurant earlier was starting to fade, so she stopped at a liquor store on the way in.

After putting the car in park right out front, she quickly ran into the store, leaving Tori in the vehicle.

"Let me get the gallon of Patron," she pointed her coffin-shaped manicured fingernail to the top shelf.

"Aye, let me get three gallons of Henny, a gallon of Patron, and I'm paying for shawty gallon too…"

Eternity turned around at the deep voice that was speaking behind her. With dark chocolate skin and chiseled features, Eternity's scowl turned into a slight smile. His locs fell at his shoulders and was neat. She looked in his eyes and wondered if he was wearing contacts. To her, there was no way that those light gray eyes could belong to him. His voice was rugged, but his features were not.

He looked like he could have been strutting down runways in Paris for a living or covering the cover of GQ magazine. His attire held a little dash of hood. The sweatsuit that he wore was simple, but the jewels on his neck and in his ears let Eternity know that the suit he wore had to cost money. Although she found the man very attractive, her days of chasing behind the dope boys were done.

"I can pay for my own bottle."

"I'm sure you can, but you shouldn't have to."

Eternity rolled her eyes. If that was his idea of a pickup line, then it was weak as fuck.

"I gotta come harder than that, huh?"

When Eternity cracked a smile, he spoke again.

"Challenge accepted."

"Who said that a challenge was even out there to be accepted?"

The man cupped his own chin with his big hand. Eternity noticed that his nails held a clear gloss. She loved a man that took care of his hygiene.

"You're right, is there?"

The smirk on his face made Eternity smile slightly.

Honk honk honk

Eternity turned towards the glass door and windows and saw Tori laying on the horn of her car. The man handed the store clerk a black card, and Eternity took notice. Money. That's what reeked from him, and it seemed as if all of the men in her life had access to that word. The same word that men would kill other grown men over.

"I guess that honking is for you, huh?" he changed the subject.

"It is," she confirmed as she took the black bag that he was handing to her.

"Damn, Cinderella, you just gone leave like that. Can I get a name?"

Eternity chuckled as she walked off and exited the store. She didn't want to let another dope boy get next to her. She had ruined Bleek, and in return, Vincent came and ruined her. Those dope boys weren't for her.

"What was taking you so long in there. I gotta pee. You know damn well when I drink, they run through me." Eternity handed Tori the black bag and then focused her attention through her windshield as she watched the man exit the liquor store and then walk towards a burgundy Denali.

"Ohhhhh, that's what was taking you so long. Damn, he looks like a model."

Tori said as she watched the six-foot two-inch frame make his way to his car.

"I hope you got his number," she added.

"I didn't"

"And whyyyyyy the fuck not?"

"Look at him. Look at that damn car. He reeks of a dope boy. *Oh, I got the bag on me. Hold on, bae, I gotta re-up.* I can hear the bullshit from now."
Tori burst into laughter. Which caused Eternity to laugh as well.

"I'm serious, don't he?"

Tori turned her head and looked as the man rolled his tinted window down. The sounds of Boozie blasted from his vehicle.

You wanna talk shit? (Talk shit)
You wanna run ya mouth? (Run ya mouth)
You want some gangsta's front yo motherfuckin' house?
We'll set this bitch off, yeah, set this bitch off

Tori laughed as he pulled off.

"Seeeeee," Eternity screeched.

"Okay, you got a point."

Tori chuckled as Eternity pulled out of the parking lot and drove in the opposite direction of the mystery man.

Chapter 17

When the Washington sisters partied, they partied hard. Tori stood on the leather sofa in their section and rapped along to a Young M.A song. The sides of the jean jacket that covered her strapless bodycon dress swayed from side to side. The burnt orange dress ended mid-calf, showing off her tattoo. The vans on her feet pressed into the leather material as she swayed from side to side.

These haters on my body shake 'em off
I could never lose what you thought? What they thought?
I could never lose what you thought?
This Henny got me, it got me sauced
This Henny got me oh, it got me sauced

"I could never lose what you thought?" Eternity joined in as she stood on the sofa next to her sister.

In her hand, she held the same gallon of Patron that the mystery man had purchased for her. She took a swig straight from the bottle as the song started to end.

"Alright y'all, this is DJ Smoove Sounds Jay, and this shoutout is to say congratulations on the return of the wide receiver for the Atlanta Falcons, Prince Bontou. Where you at boy? We knew you would heal up. We happy to see you back."

Eternity and Tori looked to the section that was diagonally from them.

"Is that?"

"The man you were calling a dope boy. Sure is. Go ahead, sis," – Tori stopped speaking to wipe Eternity's chin – "Go ahead and fix ya face and let me wipe that regret off for you."

Eternity slapped away her sister's hand and then chuckled.

"Ain't no regret, baby, watch this."

Eternity said when she noticed that Prince was walking towards the bar.

She loved how the blazer he wore hugged his broad shoulders. His locs that were at his shoulders earlier that day were now pulled up into a man bun. His straight-legged jeans hugged his toned calf, and the loafers he wore looked like they cost a pretty penny. She stood back and watched as the women at the bar flocked to him. He flashed his winning smile at some, but he didn't seem interested.

Eternity took that as a challenge. *Challenge accepted,* Eternity thought to herself. There she was quoting his same exact phrase from earlier that day. She stood back and observed him. She studied how he moved. If Bleek had taught her anything, it was to study body language. He seemed uncomfortable around the crowd that gathered around him.

Seeing enough, she decided to intervene. Lightly she placed her hand on the shoulder of the groupies as she passed by. It was her way of letting her presence be known. When Prince was given his drink and started to reach into his back pocket for his wallet, Eternity spoke loud enough for him and the drooling bartender to hear.

"I got his drink, and can you give me a nick size of Moscato, please?"

Prince turned around, and the corners of his chocolate mouth turned upward. When his gray eyes landed on her, he revealed his pearly whites.

"Awww shit, look at this, Cinderella."
Eternity chuckled at his southern drawl. It was sexy as shit to her.

"It's Eternity."

"Oh, I get a name now?" he asked as he raised his bushy eyebrow.

"Seeing you two times in one day is name worthy."

The deep chuckle that escaped his body made Eternity's knees weak. The deep grunted *mmmm* that was attached to his laugh made her wonder what he sounded like in bed. It made her wonder what love sounds he created. With toned arms, she knew that he could toss her frame around with ease. It had been so long since her body had been touched in the womanly parts that she had forgotten what an orgasm felt like.

"Well look, shawty you ain't een gotta pay for my drink. I get em for free. I was just tipping the girl. You partying by ya self or ya man around here somewhere?"

A woman standing nearby sucked her teeth. Which caught Prince's attention.

"Now I just know you ain't sucking them jibs cause I asked about shawty man? You and every chick behind you are trying too hard. Whatever Cinderella got over here come natural baby. You can gone head with da bull."
Eternity placed her hand over her mouth as she lightly chuckled.

"Don't laugh, answer the question. You here with ya man or not?"

"My name is Eternity, not Cinderella, and I'm here with my sister."

"I like Eternity, but Cinderella is special because I gave it to you. Go and get ya sister and then come to my section."

He was so close that Eternity smelt the mint scent on his breath. She got lost in his gray eyes. His request was stern but not demanding, and before she could protest, he turned on his heels and then walked away.

"Here's your wine, love."
The bartender said to Eternity as she handed the small green bottle her way.

"Don't worry about paying either. I see you're with him," she added.

Eternity made her way back to her section.

"What happened?" Tori asked as soon as Eternity took a seat next to her.

"He wants us to come to his section."

"Ohhhh, so he like you like you?"

"I mean, I guess…. Let's go."
Together the ladies walked over to Prince's section. With the congratulations in order, Eternity knew that the night would be one to remember.

Tori woke with a splitting headache. The alarm from her phone wasn't making it any better. It was time for her to get up and get ready for her flight.

"Tori Tee, wake up girl I done watched you snooze that damn alarm about four times already."

"Four times? Got damn!"

"Uh uh, stop talking, you sound a damn mess. Your voice all horse and shit."

"How is yours not after last night?" Tori asked as she rubbed the sleep out of her eyes.

"Well, while your ass was getting pissy drunk, I was sobering up, just talking and vibing with Prince."

"Ooooh, do tell, cause I don't remember shit from last night."

Tori said as she stood from the bed and stretched.

"I'll fill you in on the ride to the airport. Go and get yourself together while I pack your things."

"Fine."

Tori slowly walked to the nearby bathroom.

A car drive later...

"Do not get all watery-eyed. You're the one that only came out here for the weekend."

Tori sighed as she wiped at the tears that started to trail down her face.

"Ughhh, you're right," she agreed, "I just enjoyed my weekend with my big sis," she added.

"And there will be more weekends and times to enjoy. Your birthday is right around the corner. Do you want me to walk you in?"

"Hell no, then I'll really be crying."
Tori leaned over the middle console to give her big sister a hug.

After getting the mushy shit out of the way, Tori exited the car and then grabbed her suitcase out of the trunk.

"I love you, Tori Tee," Eternity yelled out of the car.

"I love you too, E," Tori yelled just before she entered the automatic doors.
Tori checked in for her flight, made it through security, and then waited at the gate to board. Her thumb hovered over Man-Man's name in her phone. They had gone without talking the entire weekend. He had liked her Facebook statuses as she updated them, but that was it.

Is this what they had come to? Liking statuses on
Facebook. Just when she was about to press the button to call
him, she received an incoming call. She didn't recognize the
number, so she shot the call to voicemail. When the same
number called again, she answered with much attitude.

"Hello?"

"Well, damn, could the attitude disappear or what?"

"Bleek?"

"Mean ass, Tori."

Tori smiled at the sound of his voice. The last time
she saw him was the day of her nephew's funeral. She
remembered that he said he would text her with his new
number, but here it was over nine months later, and he was
just now calling.

"Well, damn, it took you long enough to slide with
the new number."

Bleek chuckled.

"After everything that happened, I just needed to get
my mind right."

"Understandable."

There was an awkward silence. Eternity had distanced herself
from Tori for her mental state, and now Tori was discovering
that so had Bleek.

The two people she needed the most had ghosted her when she needed a check on her mental as well."

"Listen… I'm sorry for disappearing on you. I just knew you had your hands full being new to motherhood and all."

There is was—the stab in the heart. Eternity had unknowingly done it, and now so did Bleek.

"I am… well…"

Before she could say another word, tears erupted from her body. When Bleek heard gasping on the line, he spoke.

"What the fuck just happened?"

"I just… I can't talk about it right now."

"Okay, okay."

His tone softened.

"I was calling because I still have this store that's been sitting here for almost two years. It was for Eternity but…. Yeah, I just wanna know if you want it."

With the back of her hand, Tori wiped the snot from her upper lip.

"Hell yeah, I want it!"

This is exactly what she needed, a project to work on to take her mind off of everything.

"How soon can you get to Miami?" Bleek asked.

"I'm already at the airport. I can try and get a flight now."

Tori stood from her seat then walked through the airport until she reached a desk where she could buy a one-way ticket to Miami. Her and Bleek continued with their conversation as she made her way.

"What the hell are you doing in an airport already?"

"I just came from seeing Eternity."

And there it was, that awkward silence again.

"How is she?"

"She's actually doing okay."

"That's good…"

The silence came back.

"Hold on, Bleek."

After being put on hold for about five minutes, Tori came back to the phone.

"Yeah. Hello?"

"Yeah. Were you able to get a flight?"

"Yeah, I just gotta wait three hours."

"Ahhh damn, well I'll be there to pick you up from the airport just let me know what time you're supposed to land."

"Okay, well, while I wait, I can tell you everything that you missed with me."

Bleek chuckled as he kicked his sneakers off. He knew that Tori would find some way to bring the conversation back to catching him up. After leaning back onto his couch with his arms spread on the back of it, he spoke.

"Aight baby girl, catch me up."

Chapter 18

After the long conversation with Tori, Bleek found himself sprawled across his comforter on his bed lying next to Paris. He just needed his body to rest a little before he went to the airport to pick Tori up.

"You have to get into the groove of social media, babe."
Bleek huffed as he continued to swipe across the screen of his phone.

"Malikkk…" she whined.

"What?" he answered, never looking up from his phone.

Tony: Get on a flight so we can discuss Chiva Blanca in person. I've made an interesting discovery.

Bleek quickly read over the text that had his attention, and then he locked his phone. He gave Paris his attention.

"If you are serious about opening an MB's Auto in Miami Beach, then you have to get down with social media. Having a shop in Fort Lauderdale and having one in Miami Beach is a different ball game." She paused her rant when she noticed Bleek's screwed facial expression. "Fix your face. The younger crowd is big on social media. All these teenagers are getting their first cars and not keeping up with them. You can be that voice on social media that shows them how to take care of these cars."

"Fine," Bleek finally broke, "set it up."

He kissed her on the side of her head and then stood from the bed.

"Wait, set it up?" she questioned.

"Yeah, you're big on social media. Get us started." Paris smiled brightly. Her own career was just now starting to take off. With help from her father, she was sitting in on law cases that she probably would not have seen until her fifth year on the job. So, she knew that she couldn't run the social media for his business forever, but having a hand in it meant that they were elevating in their relationship. In a sense, he was now trusting her with his financials.

"I'll get it started, but let me be in charge of hiring someone for social media. This isn't something that I can do forever."

"Okay, get it done," Bleek said as he quickly dressed.

The way he said *get it done* in that tone made her want to jump all over him. He was a self-made boss, and the way he carried himself drove her crazy. She frowned when she saw him go into his closet and put on the same sneakers he had just put in there not too long ago.

"Where are you going?" Paris asked.

"I need to go pick up my little sis from the airport."

"You have a little sister?"

"Yeah."

There was still so much that she didn't know about Malik Browne. They had been dealing for a while now and as to why she didn't know that he had a sister was beyond her. She didn't know that Ty wasn't Bleek's real brother, and she never had any intentions of questioning it.

She smiled inwardly at the thought of meeting his little sister. Instantly the feeling of wondering if the girl would like her crossed her mind. She hadn't met much of his family, and the only family that she did meet, she ended up getting off on the wrong foot. Luckily, she was able to clean that up, but she knew that little sisters were special. Most little sisters held the key to their big brother's heart, so she knew that her first impression had to be a good one.

"Will she be staying here with us?"

Us? Bleek tilted his head and then looked at her. There was no blaming her for this newfound attachment to his home because he had allowed her to be over daily. Ever since his condo had been ransacked in connection with this Chiva Blanca person, they had been held up at his home.

"I don't know yet, but uh, I'ma need a few days alone with her, aight?"

"Oh. Okay…"

Paris eyebrows raised as she grabbed the iPad off the nightstand and then stood from the bed.

"Where are you going?" Bleek asked as he crossed his muscular arms across his broad chest.

"I'm about to go home. It makes no sense in me being here by the time you get back with her."

"Paris—"

"No, it's okay, really."

Bleek knew that Paris was an emotional being, so he knew that she probably took his words the wrong way, and that wasn't his intention. He just knew that he didn't want to parade another woman around Tori. Especially on her first day into town. He knew that a formal introduction had to be made between the two ladies.

He respected Tori just as he would Eternity because well, she was an extension to the love of his life. Bleek rolled his neck around and then sighed when he saw Paris step her bare feet into her Uggs. Her pajama pants laid over the top of the boot messily.

"You don't have to leave right now at this moment."

"Na, it's cool. I'll head home and then start on the Instagram account and Facebook like page for the shop, okay?"

Gently she kissed Bleek's cheek in passing.

"Yo."

He grabbed her arm and then pulled her back to him. He held the back of her neck and then smashed their lips together.

"Chill out, you here."

He knew that she was overthinking that sexy ass mind of hers. A slight smile crept across her face.

"After you get your sister settled in, you can put your key to use." She said with a wink before she exited the room.

"Na, after I get my sister settled, you can put *your key* to use," he countered.

He followed her down the stairs, and together, they walked out of his front door. He opened the door to her white Mercedes Benz for her and waited for her to get in before he gently closed the door behind her. She backed out of his driveway and then took off. The only woman before Paris that was privileged to be inside of his home was Eternity.

Because of the current circumstances, he had her there. His apartment wasn't safe, and he wouldn't have her in harm's way. Besides caring about her deeply, he knew that her dad wouldn't have it if anything was to happen to her. Bleek got into his Tesla and then backed out of his driveway. He looked at the time on the dashboard and saw that he was still on time to get Tori.

Bleek drove in silence as he made his way to the airport. It reminded him of when he went to pick Eternity up from the airport. He was driving the same car, taking the same roads. The only difference was that he was now driving to pick up Tori.

Just like her sister, she was coming his way while her world was turned upside down. He wondered how she was mentally. Still, he thought of Eternity. He knew that him basically taking in Tori could possibly bring Eternity out of hiding. But then again, it had been months, and he hadn't heard from her.

Over the months, he had half of mind to use his resources to his advantage to find her, but he decided not to because he knew that this space that she was taking was very much needed. Still, the thoughts of knowing if she was even okay consumed the fuck out of him. That was until Tori confirmed that she was just fine. If she was to come out of hiding, he honestly didn't know what he would do.

Things with he and Paris felt good. She gave him the security that he had been seeking his whole life. He was starting to love her, and the feeling was killing him. Still, even with the growing feeling of love, his devotion to Eternity hadn't wavered. Paris was everything and more, but to Bleek, she just wasn't Eternity.

Bleek quickly pulled over and then parked when he saw Tori waltz out of the airport.

"Brotherrrrr…." Tori ran to Bleek full speed.

He leaned up against the side of his car to brace himself. Her eyes were filled with tears, and when their bodies collided, the trails cascaded down her flushed face. He didn't know how she was still standing. In order, she lost her nephew, her boyfriend was shot, her sister voluntarily went missing, she had lost her own child, and then she discovered that the same boyfriend that she had nursed back to health had been unfaithful.

In his embrace, Bleek felt Tori's back heaving up and down.

"Aight yo, You good. You hear me? You good." He reassured.

"When I needed my sister, she wasn't there. I just spent an entire weekend with her, and I didn't get that off my chest."

Bleek knew that he was secondary to Tori's troubles. What she really needed back then was her big sister. He broke their embrace and then gave her a weak smile.

"She's back now, though, and I got you, aight?"

Her brown orbs looked into his eyes, and still, she couldn't stop crying.

"How could he do that to me and be so regular now?" She said out loud, although she was wondering it to herself. Her thoughts jumped from her big sister to the man she had left behind.

Bleek clenched his jaw repeatedly. That protector instinct that was embedded in him started to surface. The simple fact that Man-Man had gotten caught out there doing her dirty after she had lost their child had totally slipped his mind. She didn't request a hit, so he wasn't going to offer. He was tired of getting stains on his damn resume. But whenever she had a change of mind and wanted him handled, he would make sure that the job got done.

"Fuck that. His loss, right? That's what big sisters are supposed to say, right? Is this what E was saying all weekend? Fuck that nigga girlll he was a loser anyway…" he said the last part in a girly voice that caused Tori to start laughing.

He quickly hugged her again and then chuckled himself. He could tell that he would love having her around because it would be like having Eternity around. Still, he yearned for her. So being in the presence of her replica would be a good substitution for now.

"You gone be good. I'ma keep you busy aight?"

Tori sniffled, wiped her nose with the back of her hand, and then smiled.

"Where are your bags?" he asked when he realized that only a purse was on her forearm.

"My little suitcase is coming later. I think they sent it back to Chattanooga first since I changed my flight last minute."

"I got you on that too..." Bleek took his wallet out of his pocket and then gave her a credit card from it.

"Come on, let's go." He added as he opened the passenger side door for her.

After making sure that she was tucked away safely, he rounded the car and then got in on the driver's side. As he drove them both to his home, he thought about how he had to get Tori settled before he took another trip to D.R. He had to finally get to the bottom of Chiva Blanca.

"I gotta go outta town for a couple of days. I'ma put you in touch with Sha, aight? He'll show you around. You remember him, right?"

"Yeah, that's the one that came to Chattanooga with you, right?"

"Yeah, that's him."

The rest of the ride to his house was silent. Tori sat on the other side of the car, wondering how her life had gotten to this point. Bleek had too much on his mind to sort through it all. Together they were two broken souls that were just trying to get it all together again.

$\mathcal{C}$hapter 19

Tori lightly strutted down the driveway. She had finally gotten settled into Bleek's home. Before he left to go handle his business in D.R, he had set Tori up with Sha's number. She needed to go shopping, and he was the one that was going to take her.

When she got into the car, he backed out the driveway and then made his way to Lincoln Road Mall. The silence in the car was killing Tori. Lightly the radio in the back played, but that wasn't enough for her. She wanted human interaction.

"So, Sha, right? Where are we going first?"

"First?" Sha took his eyes off of the road to quickly glance in her direction.

"Man, we going to one mall, and you gone get whatever it is that you need from there."

Tori sucked her teeth and then crossed her arms over her breast.

"For all of that, I could have used GPS on my phone and drove my damn self around."

"Yeah, you really could have, but my boy asked me to do something. So, here I am."

Sha used the button on his steering wheel to turn his radio up.

I'm coming back for good
So let them niggas know it's mines
I already got someone is what you tell 'em every time
That shit ain't up for grabs
Where you at on the map
I come to where you at
Fuck around and end up your last
I won't hold back

Tori sat back in her chair and listened to the soft sounds of Bryson Tiller. Looking at the rugged appearance of Sha she expected someone like DMX to be on his playlist. She didn't doubt that he had a song or two of his on the playlist, but she could tell that he enjoyed the softer music as well.

She glanced over at him and took in his hardy features. His beard was lined perfectly, and his thick sideburns attached to his beard perfectly. The beard fell off his face four inches and looked soft to the touch. His hair was low cut and wavy.

His brown skin looked tanned, and Tori just knew that the Florida sun that constantly beamed down on him had to have a hand in that. At a light, he turned her way. His untamed bushy eyebrows scrunched. He turned the music down.

"What you looking at?"

"Nothing."

Tori quickly turned her head.

"Oh… aight."

Tori snapped her head in his direction and then sucked her teeth. *Oh, I know this Floridian did not just hit me with a New York ass "oh, aight."* She thought.

"Uh, uh! Mr. Rude Ass."

He chuckled at her slight attitude as he was pulling into a parking space near the shopping center entrance. After parking, he killed the engine.

"What ya rude ass turning the car off for? You can just drop me and go."

"Girl, I need to get myself some shit."

"Yeah, well where are we meeting and at what time so I can know how much time I have to shop?"

"Na, little miss, we are sticking together while we go in and out of these stores. You not about to leave my side and disappear somewhere."

"Fuck you think I'm a child?" she asked.

He didn't say anything because he thought of her sister. Eternity had up and left everyone behind, and there was no way that he would lower his guard and Tori take off under his supervision. There was no explaining that to Bleek.

"Like I said, we're sticking together."
Tori sucked her teeth and then opened the car door. Sha was giving her big brother vibes, and she hated it. She hated being micromanaged and hawked, but what else was she to expect if she was now relocated with Bleek.

He would always have that protector instinct, so she knew that the men around him would be the same way. Bleek only aligned and surrounded himself with men that were the same caliber of him, and she knew that. She didn't know how Ty had slipped through the cracks because, to her, he was the furthest thing from trustworthy and honest, but he was Bleek's family.

As soon as the pair walked into the shopping area, Tori made her way towards Victoria's secret.

"I know you don't want to bring your ass in here with me."

"Yeah, na. Go ahead and handle your business. I'm gonna be in the Foot Action right there across the pathway."

Tori smiled brightly and then started her way into the underwear shop. As she walked past the aisles, she fanned her hand over the silk robes that were on hangers.

"Those are nice. Get the blue one. It would look nice on your skin."

Tori turned around and was faced with one of the prettiest smiles she had ever seen in her life. She held back her slight smile with a compelling look. She wondered what this man was doing inside of the store. She didn't see a woman around him, and if he didn't work there, then in her mind, he was a creep.

"Thanks for your suggestion, but maybe you should finish shopping for your wife." She said once she looked down at his hand and noticed the silver wedding band that dressed his hand.

She turned back around to the rack and then went to the red robes and looked for her size. It seemed like she was the magnet for married men. Every single man that had approached her in the last five years all had someone at home, and then there was Man-Man.

She had met him when he was out of his situation, only to later be slapped in the face with the infidelities of him and the same wife he had left. At this point, she pondered with the thought of playing on the other team, but she could never see herself face down in between a woman's legs, so she quickly got that idea out of her head.

𝒞hapter 20

It was coming to the weekend of Tori's birthday, and Eternity had made it up in her mind that she was going to do a surprise visit to see Tori for her special day. She had mentioned it when she had last saw her, but they hadn't discussed it lately. After calling Tori's number and not getting an answer, she tried another number where she knew Tori could be reached.

The ringing in Eternity's ear was dragging, and just when she was going to hang up, a woman answered.

"Hello?"

Stunned that the woman's voice didn't belong to her sister, Eternity hesitated with a response.

"Hello?" the woman asked again.

"Can I speak to Marcelo?"

"Who's asking?"

Eternity cocked her head to the side because the woman answering her sister's house phone had a lot of nerve.

This better be the maid or something, Eternity thought to herself.

"Ummm, where is my sister?" Eternity's patience was growing short."

"No woman lives here to be receiving calls here."

"Okay, enough is enough. Where the fuck is Marcelo?"

"This is my fucking hou—"

"Nova!"

Eternity heard Marcelo's deep voice in the background. She listened to the woman remove her ear, and then she was greeted with Man-Man's raspy one.

"Hello?"

"Marcelo, there better be a damn good reason as to why another bitch is answering the phone there where my sister lives."

"Eternity?"

"Mmmm hmmm."

"For one, your sister doesn't live here anymore. She sent me some long ass text three weeks ago saying how she couldn't do this anymore. I thought she was still out there with you."

"Well, she isn't." Eternity said flatly.

"Well, then, I don't know. I honestly think her leaving without an explanation was unnecessary, so where she is now is not my problem."

Eternity screwed her face terribly. *The nerve of these niggas,* she thought to herself. How dare he utter from those deceiving lips that Tori left without explanation when he had stayed out all night without one. The old her would have told him the fuck off. Her words were lethal, and for her sister, she would spit deadly hot venom that'll make the most secure nigga want to kill himself.

"Enjoy your life. I really hope you do know that my sister was the best bitch you could have ever gotten."

Before he could say anything in return, Eternity hung up her phone. For a while, Eternity sat with her phone in her hand. She was debating on how she should approach the situation with her sister. Since Tori had left, she let Eternity know when she was home. They had texted just this morning, and Tori said that she was home. *If she isn't in Chattanooga, then where the fuck is she?* Eternity thought to herself.

Tori woke out of her bed to the smell of breakfast. The luxurious one-bedroom suite with the attached bathroom is what Bleek offered to her. The closet was just as big as the bathroom and now filled thanks to Bleek's card and the shopping trip that Sha had chaperoned.

After brushing her teeth and putting on her pajama pants, she made her way down to the kitchen. Before leaving on his trip, Bleek formally introduced Tori to Paris. Now that he was gone, the space in the home was awkward.

"I made some breakfast if you want some. I'm going to get Malik from the airport in a little bit."
Tori screwed her face at Paris' chipper demeanor, sat at a stool, reached into the bowl that stood on the kitchen island, and then took a red apple from it.

"Na, I'm good."

Tori said just before she rubbed the apple on her pajama top to clean it and then took a bite. Paris picked up a piece of turkey bacon from a nearby plate and then took a bite.

"It's really good," she said out loud.
Tori didn't say anything because she didn't care for Paris much. To her, it was like the girl tried too hard. Bleek introduced Tori as his sister, and Paris had been kissing ass ever since.

Tori already had it made up in her mind that she would never get too close to Paris. Her blood sister was Bleek's past love, so befriending Paris was a no-no. She didn't care that Bleek had moved on with Paris or that Eternity was seeming to move on with Prince. In her eyes, she would always be team Eternity and Bleek.

Tori watched as Paris picked at the scrambled eggs on her plate.

"Would you like to come with me to get him from the airport?"

"Yeah, that's cool."

Paris' eyes lit up.

"Okay, we can leave in like thirty minutes."

"Aight."

Tori tossed the stem and center of the apple in the nearby garbage and then went to her room to get ready.

Tori watched out the side of her eye as Paris tapped the steering wheel and lightly hummed along to the music that was playing on the radio. Tori's phone began to ring, so Paris reached to turn down the music.

"Nah, you can leave the music," Tori said to Paris when she realized that it was Eternity calling her.

Paris left the volume of the radio to where it was and then continued to drive.

"Hello?" Tori answered.

"Where are you?" Eternity got straight to the point.

"Out and about. About to go back home soon."

"Funny how you say home, and I just called your house phone to get told that you don't live there anymore."

Tori remained silent.

"Oh… cat got that tongue huh? Where are you, Tori Tee?"

"I'm in Miami."

"In Miami?" – Eternity paused – *"you're with Bleek, aren't you?"*

"Uhhh yeah…"

"Okay… I mean, I get it. He's like a big brother to you."

"Yeah, he is."

The phone fell silent.

"Well, I'm coming out there for your birthday. I'll book my hotel and flight when we get off the phone."

"You're coming here?"

"Yes, I am. Look, it's been a while since he and I have talked. I'm sure he has moved on just like I'm trying to do."

"Yeah…"

And there the confirmation was. Tori was letting it be known that Bleek had indeed moved on. This new Eternity wanted him to be happy. Their love was profound, but the makings of everything surrounding their love story was also very toxic.

"When I get there, we can just chill out in the city. I can take you to the spa, and we can just have a sister weekend."

"Okay, that sounds goo—"

"He's coming out of the doors right now!" Paris said, unable to hide her excitement.

She then jumped out of the driver's seat and rounded the car to meet Bleek halfway.

"Sis, let me call you back a little later, okay?"

"Okay, I'll text you my flight and hotel information once it's booked."

"Okay," Tori responded as she got out the car to get into the back seat.

"I love you, Tori Tee."

"Love you too sis."

Tori hung up her phone, watched Paris embrace Bleek, and then she got into the back seat. Bleek and Paris got into the car together. Bleek turned around in his seat to face Tori. She smiled at him. He held a glow over his chocolate skin that only the hot Dominican Republic sun could give.

"Were my two favorite ladies playing well in the sandbox?"

Bleek made eye contact with Tori when he asked his question.

"Yes, we sure were babe," Paris said proudly. Tori silently mocked Paris and then stuck her tongue out, which caused Bleek to erupt into laughter.

Be nice, he mouthed to Tori. She rolled her eyes, so he playfully swatted at her knee before turning around in his seat. Bleek put his hand on top of the middle console, and when Paris took her hand and intertwined her fingers within Bleek's, Tori felt sick to her stomach.

She pulled her phone out and then texted the only person that could pull her from being annoyed with the stink ass attitude that she currently had.

Hey you

: What you want?

To get my mind off shit here

Tori smiled after she sent the smirking emoji after her text.

: Ha! Pull up later then.

Tori left the message on read and then sat back in the seat with a sly smirk on her face. She had found the perfect sexy distraction to keep her mind off of things, and in a few days, she would start the work on her new Beauty Bar: Nalah's Color Box. Everything was beginning to look up for her. Her sister was coming to town, and she just knew that shit was about to shake up...

To be continued in:

A Love Affair for Eternity 4: The Finale

LEAVE THOSE REVIEWS

A Love Affair for Eternity BOOK 3

Follow C. Wilson on social media

Instagram: @authorcwilson

Facebook: @CelesteWilson

Join my reading group on Facebook: Cecret Discussionz

Follow my reading group on Instagram: @CecretDiscussionz

Twitter: @Authorcwilson_

~~~~~~~~~~~~~~~~~~~~~~~~~~~~~~~~~~

Tell me what you think of this story in a customer review.

Thank you,

-xoxo-

C. Wilson